image comics presents

NewHolly Library

APR 1_ 2017

ROBERT KIRKMAN
CREATOR, WRITER

CHARLIE ADLARD
PENCILER, INKER

CLIFF RATHBURN
GRAY TONES

RUS WOOTON
LETTERER

CHARLIE ADLARD
&
CLIFF RATHBURN
COVER

SINA GRACE
EDITOR

IMAGE COMICS, INC.

Robert Kirkman - chief operating officer
Erik Larsen - chief financial officer
Todd McFarlane - president
Marc Silvestri - chief executive officer
Jim Valentino - vice-president

Eric Stephenson - publisher
Todd Martinez - sales & licensing coordinator
Betsy Gomez - pr & marketing coordinator
Branwyn Bigglestone - accounts manager
Sarah deLaine - administrative assistant
Tyler Shainline - production manager
Drew Gill - art director
Jonathan Chan - production artist
Monica Howard - production artist
Vincent Kukua - production artist
Kevin Yuen - production artist
www.imagecomics.com

For SKYBOUND ENTERTAINMENT

Robert Kirkman - CEO
J.J. Didde - President
Sina Grace - Editorial Director
Chad Manion - Assistant to Mr. Grace

WWW.SKYBOUNDENT.COM

THE WALKING DEAD, VOL. 12: LIFE AMONG THEM. Second Printing. Published by Image Comics, Inc. Office of publication: 2134 Allston Way, 2nd Floor, Berkeley, California 94704.

Copyright © 2010 Robert Kirkman. All rights reserved.

Originally published in single magazine format as THE WALKING DEAD #67-72.

THE WALKING DEAD™ (including all prominent characters featured in this issue), its logo and all character likenesses are trademarks of Robert Kirkman, unless otherwise noted. Image Comics® and its logos are registered trademarks and copyrights of Image Comics, Inc. All rights reserved. No part of this publication may be reproduced or transmitted, in any form or by any means (except for short excerpts for review purposes) without the express written permission of Image Comics, Inc. All names, characters, events and locales in this publication are entirely fictional. Any resemblance to actual persons (living and/or dead), events or places, without satiric intent, is coincidental.

PRINTED IN THE U.S.A. For information regarding the CPSIA on this printed material call: 203-595-3636 and provide reference # EAST – 68205

ISBN: 978-1-60706-254-7

FUCK.

GO BACK!
GO BACK!

HOW MANY IS IT?
SHH!

YOU DON'T WANT TO KNOW. LET'S JUST GET OUT OF HERE.

DID THEY HEAR US? THE LEAVES?

I DON'T KNOW FOR SURE, BEST WE JUST KEEP MOVING EITHER WAY.
IT'S PAST TIME FOR US TO BE GETTING BACK, ANYWAY.

I HOPE EVERYONE FOUND MORE FOOD THAN US. I HATE OATMEAL.
SOMETIMES I HAVE A HARD TIME KEEPING TRACK OF THE FOOD YOU DON'T HATE.

I MISS CHEESE-BURGERS.

REMEMBER PIZZA?

SO... WE HAVEN'T HAD A LOT OF TIME TO OURSELVES THESE PAST FEW WEEKS...
...NO CHANCE TO TALK.

WHY DID YOU KILL BEN?

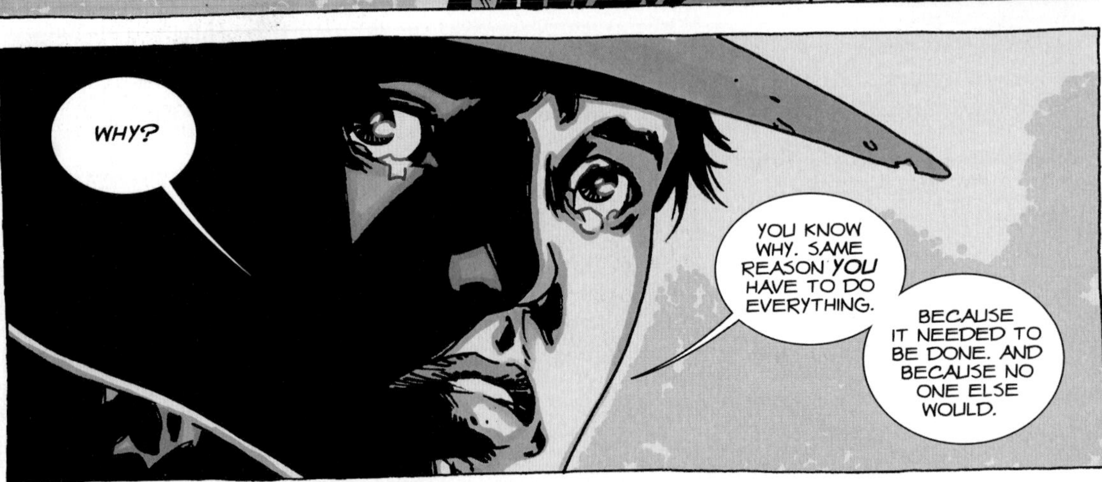
WHY?
YOU KNOW WHY. SAME REASON *YOU* HAVE TO DO EVERYTHING.
BECAUSE IT NEEDED TO BE DONE. AND BECAUSE NO ONE ELSE WOULD.

I DO THINGS... A LOT OF *BAD* THINGS, TO HELP YOU AND ALL THE OTHER PEOPLE IN OUR GROUP.
AND AS YOU GROW UP, YOU'LL PROBABLY HAVE TO DO THAT TOO. THAT'S THE WORLD WE LIVE IN NOW... BUT CARL, YOU NEED TO NEVER FORGET...
WHEN WE DO THESE THINGS AND WE'RE GOOD PEOPLE... THEY'RE STILL *BAD* THINGS.

YOU CAN NEVER LOSE SIGHT OF THAT. IF THESE THINGS START BECOMING *EASY* THAT'S WHEN IT'S ALL OVER.
THAT'S WHEN WE BECOME BAD PEOPLE.

I CRY EVERY NIGHT.
I USUALLY SNEAK AWAY, AFTER YOU'RE ASLEEP. I DON'T WANT YOU TO HEAR IT. I DIDN'T WANT YOU TO WORRY ABOUT ME.
I HAVE TROUBLE SOMETIMES DURING THE DAY, KEEPING MYSELF FROM CRYING. IT'S *HARD.*
I REMEMBER THE LOOK HE HAD ON HIS FACE. HE DIDN'T WANT TO HURT ME.
IT WAS LIKE HE WANTED TO PLAY WITH ME. HE WAS HAPPY TO SEE ME. HE ASKED ME IF I WAS AFRAID OF HIM.

I THINK HE WAS WORRIED THAT I WOULDN'T PLAY WITH HIM ANYMORE.
I *LIKED* BEN.
HE--
HE WAS MY *FRIEND.*

I MISS HIM. I SEE HIM WHEN I CLOSE MY EYES AND I REMEMBER HIM LIKE HE WAS, BEFORE HE DID WHAT HE DID-- BEFORE HE KILLED BILLY.
I KNOW WHAT I DID WAS WRONG.
HE WASN'T GOING TO KILL ME, NOT RIGHT THEN. BUT I HEARD YOU TALKING, I AGREED WITH EVERYTHING YOU AND ABRAHAM SAID.
HE WAS DANGEROUS.
SON...
I WAS NEVER GOING TO TELL YOU. I'M STRONG, I CAN HANDLE THIS, DAD. I CAN.
BUT YOU SAID YOU THOUGHT I WOULDN'T LOVE YOU ANYMORE IF I KNEW WHAT YOU DID TO THOSE PEOPLE THAT HURT DALE.

I LOVE YOU BECAUSE OF WHAT YOU DO TO KEEP ME SAFE.
I KNOW WHY WE DO WHAT WE DO. WE DO IT TO PROTECT THE WEAK. TO SURVIVE.

YOU AND ABRAHAM KNEW WHAT NEEDED TO BE DONE... BUT YOU COULDN'T DO IT. YOU COULDN'T KILL A KID.
I DIDN'T WANT TO KILL BEN.
I HAD TO.

I'M SORRY, CARL.

I'M SO SORRY.

...I RAN INTO ONE. I JUST PUSHED IT OVER AND WALKED AWAY. I DON'T EVEN SEE THE POINT OF KILLING THEM ANYMORE.
FOR A WHILE IT WAS... Y'KNOW, CLEANING UP THE WORLD OR SOMETHING... I FELT LIKE I NEEDED TO KILL THEM.
BUT NOW...

...WHAT'S THE POINT?
I HOPE YOU GUYS FARED BETTER THAN WE DID.

DAMN IT, *REALLY?!*

WE GOT OUR HOPES UP-- FIGURED YOU WERE TAKING LONGER BECAUSE YOU FOUND SOMETHING.

WE FOUND *SOMETHING.* JUST NOT A LOT OF IT.
I HOPE YOU ALL LIKE OATMEAL.

WE ALSO FOUND SOME CANS OF SOUP, JUST TWO. AND A BOTTLE OF WATER, BUT IT'S BEEN OPENED.

WE FOUND SOME PEANUT BUTTER CRACKERS, BUT IT LOOKS LIKE A MOUSE CHEWED ON THE WRAPPER, SO THOSE WILL BE RESERVED FOR THE *BRAVER* AMONG US.
MICHONNE SCORED SOME FRUIT COCKTAIL AND A FEW OTHER CANS FROM A HOUSE SHE FOUND.
THAT'S ABOUT IT.

WELL, THE GOOD NEWS IS WE'RE NOT OUT OF FOOD YET. WE STILL HAVE ALL THAT RICE WE FOUND LAST WEEK.
WE'VE BOUGHT OURSELVES SOME TIME.

WHOEVER WANTS IT IS WELCOME TO *MY* OATMEAL.
YUCK!

EUGENE, WHEN'S THE LAST TIME YOU CHECKED THE RADIO?
HUH? A DAY, MAYBE TWO? WHY DO YOU ASK?

WE'VE BEEN MAKING GOOD TIME, WE'RE ALMOST TO MARYLAND... I THOUGHT IT MIGHT BE WORTH IT TO TRY IT AGAIN.

NO, WE NEED TO CONSERVE THE BATTERY. WE SHOULD WAIT AT LEAST ANOTHER DAY.

BUT WE'RE GETTING SO MUCH CLOSER TO WASHINGTON. WE'RE ALMOST THERE. A FEW DAYS AWAY AT MOST. HOW MUCH BATTERY DO WE NEED?

IS IT STILL IN THE CAB OF THE TRUCK? I'LL DO IT. I JUST WANT TO TURN IT ON REAL QUICK, ZIP THROUGH THE BAND, SEE IF WE CAN FIND ANYTHING. MAYBE SEND OUT A MESSAGE.
C'MON.
NO, WAIT!

RICK, STOP!

I CAN DO IT.
I WANT TO FOOL AROUND WITH IT. DAMN IT, EUGENE! WHAT ARE YOU DOING?

SERIOUSLY, WHAT THE HELL?! ARE YOU CRAZY?!
IT'S DELICATE-- I CAN'T HAVE YOU BREAKING IT. LET GO!

GUYS-- WHAT THE HELL?
THIS IS--

LET--!

WRAKK!

KRAKK!

NOW LOOK WHAT YOU DID!
YOU FUCKING BROKE IT!

WHY ISN'T THERE A BATTERY INSIDE?

THE BATTERY RAN OUT A FEW WEEKS AGO, I DIDN'T WANT TO WORRY ANYONE.
I TOOK IT OUT SO IT WOULDN'T CORRODE THE RADIO.

YOU DIDN'T THINK THIS WOULD BE SOMETHING WORTH TELLING US?!

WAIT.

HOW LONG AGO DID THE BATTERY *REALLY* DIE?

WERE THERE *EVER* BATTERIES IN IT?

WHAT?

NO.
NEVER.

YOU MOTHER FUCKER!
WRAMM!
HUWAAGH!

IS THAT WHERE THE LIES END?!
WERE YOU REALLY A SCIENTIST?! DID YOU REALLY WORK FOR THE GOVERNMENT?!
TELL ME!
ABRAHAM, DON'T HURT HIM!

HIGH SCHOOL--
SCIENCE--
TEACHER...
WHAT THE FUCK?!
KRAK!!
OKAY, STOP-- I'M NOT GOING TO LET YOU KILL HIM!
CALM DOWN!
YOU DON'T KNOW WHAT I'VE BEEN THROUGH-- KEEPING THIS SACK OF SHIT ALIVE!
AND FOR WHAT?!
I'VE TRAVELED ACROSS THE GODDAMN COUNTRY FOR HIM! HE TOLD US WASHINGTON WAS SAFE--RUNNING JUST LIKE NORMAL.
PEOPLE HAVE DIED BECAUSE OF HIM--BECAUSE I THOUGHT IT WAS IMPORTANT TO GET HIM TO WASHINGTON!
WHY, GOD DAMN IT?!
WHY?!

I ONLY DID...
...WHAT I *HAD* TO DO.
I'M NOT STRONG.
I CAN'T GET BY ON MY LOOKS.
I'M NOT SOME GREAT LEADER.
I'M NOT BRAVE.
I'M NOT USEFUL.

I HAVE TWO THINGS GOING FOR ME.
I AM EXTREMELY INTELLIGENT.
AND I AM A GOOD LIAR.
I DIDN'T HAVE A LOT OF OPTIONS.

I WAS SCARED...
SO SCARED...

I'M VERY SORRY.

STILL PISSED?
YEAH, BUT NOT AT *HIM.*

I LED A BUNCH OF PEOPLE TO THEIR DEATHS FOR THAT GUY.
A LOT OF PEOPLE ARE DEAD BECAUSE OF ME.

TRUST ME, IF YOU LOOK AT THINGS THAT WAY, YOU'LL DRIVE YOURSELF CRAZY.
AND IT'S JUST AS EASY TO CONVINCE YOURSELF THAT OTHER PEOPLE ARE ALIVE BECAUSE OF YOU.

THEY JUST WANTED SOME FOOD--BUT I THOUGHT THE MISSION WAS SO IMPORTANT. MORE IMPORTANT THAN ANYTHING...
I COULDN'T RISK NOT MAKING IT TO WASHINGTON...

...*CHRIST.*

SO...

SO?

SO WHAT DO WE DO **NOW?**

WE'RE ONLY ABOUT A FEW DAYS OUT OF WASHINGTON. DO WE STILL GO?
WHAT'S THE POINT?
WE'RE OUT OF FOOD--IF THE CITIES WERE THE FIRST TO FALL--AND ARE DENSELY INFESTED WITH ROAMERS, THAT'S GOING TO BE THE MOST LIKELY PLACE TO HAVE FOOD.
I SAY WE STILL GO. WE MIGHT AS WELL.

HE MAY NOT HAVE KNOWN IT, BUT EUGENE COULD HAVE BEEN RI--
EXCUSE ME...

...COULD ONE OF YOU POINT ME TO WHOEVER IS IN CHARGE OF THIS LITTLE GROUP?

THE BOSS. WHOEVER IS CALLING THE SHOTS.
I'D REALLY LIKE TO SPEAK WITH THEM.

MY NAME IS **AARON.** I'M NOT HERE TO FIGHT. I DON'T HAVE ANY WEAPONS.
SERIOUSLY. JUST WANT TO TALK. COOL?

WHERE DID YOU COME FROM? WERE YOU WATCHING US?

FULL DISCLOSURE? ***YEP.***
BUT I WAS JUST LISTENING TO YOU GUYS TALK... JUST TO MAKE SURE YOU WEREN'T DANGEROUS OR ANYTHING.

WROKK!

WHU

JUST SO WE'RE CLEAR. THAT WAS NOT A "LET'S ATTACK THIS MAN" LOOK.
THAT WAS A "SEEMS LIKE AN OKAY GUY TO ME" LOOK.

I'M CONFUSED.
I DON'T CARE IF HE DIDN'T HAVE WEAPONS. I DON'T CARE IF HE'S ALONE. HE'S NOT SURVIVED THIS LONG ALONE. AND I DON'T KNOW ABOUT YOU, BUT FROM MY EXPERIENCE, PEOPLE ARE DANGEROUS.
I SEE SOMEONE WHO'S OVERLY FRIENDLY, AND I SEE THE GOVERNOR. THAT GUY WAS ALL SMILES WHEN WE MET HIM.

HELP ME TIE HIM UP.

HE'S WAKING UP.

UNGH.

GUESS THAT MAKES YOU THE LEADER, THEN?
CAN I GET YOUR NAME?

MY NAME IS RICK, AND YOU'RE GOING TO ANSWER ALL OF MY QUESTIONS.
NO EXCEPTIONS.

THAT'S WHY I'M HERE. TO TALK.
WE COULD HAVE DONE THIS WITHOUT THE VIOLENCE, RICK. BUT I KNOW WHA IT'S LIKE OUT HERE. TRUST AIN'T EASY.
I DON' HOLD IT AGAINS YOU.

GOOD MAN. I APPRECIATE THAT.
HOW MANY PEOPLE ARE IN YOUR GROUP?

I DON'T KNOW, THIRTY-FOUR OR SO. I THINK WE'RE STILL UNDER FORTY.

THAT MANY? WHERE ARE THEY?

IN OUR COMMUNITY, IT'S ON THE OTHER SIDE OF D.C. ABOUT TWENTY MILES AWAY.
WHY ARE YOU *HERE?*

I'M A KIND OF RECRUITER, I GUESS. I PROMISE I WAS ONLY SPYING ON YOU TO MAKE SURE THAT YOUR GROUP WOULD... FIT IN? I THINK THAT'S WHAT I MEAN TO SAY.
BEEN WATCHING YOU FOR A WHILE. YOU SEEM LIKE A NICE BUNCH OF FOLKS. THE KID DOESN'T LIKE OATMEAL. IT'S FUNNY.
I KNOW YOU'RE HAVING TROUBLE FINDING FOOD--THAT'S COMMON AROUND HERE. WE'VE PRETTY MUCH EXHAUSTED ALL THE SUPPLIES IN THIS AREA.
WE HAVE STOCKPILES OF FOOD. WE HAVE SECURITY WALLS. WE HAVE ROOM FOR ALL OF YOU. I PROMISE YOU, OUR COMMUNITY IS EVERYTHING YOU'VE BEEN LOOKING FOR.
I'M HERE TO INVITE YOU TO... AUDITION FOR MEMBERSHIP.

YOU'VE GOT A SAFE, SECURE PLACE TO LIVE AND YOU'RE JUST TRAVELING AROUND INVITING PEOPLE IN?
WHAT'S IN IT FOR *YOU?*

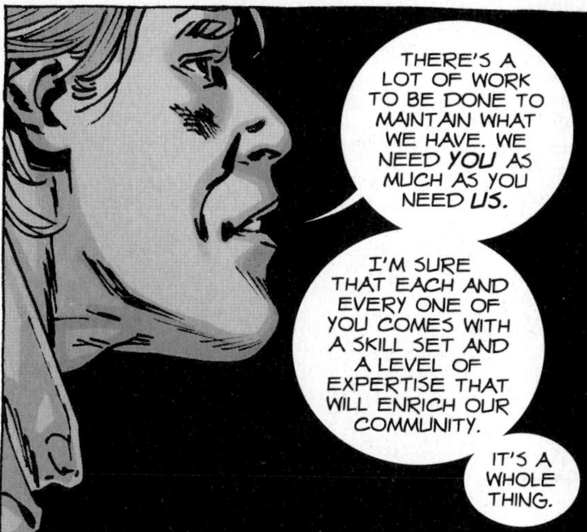
THERE'S A LOT OF WORK TO BE DONE TO MAINTAIN WHAT WE HAVE. WE NEED *YOU* AS MUCH AS YOU NEED *US.*
I'M SURE THAT EACH AND EVERY ONE OF YOU COMES WITH A SKILL SET AND A LEVEL OF EXPERTISE THAT WILL ENRICH OUR COMMUNITY.
IT'S A WHOLE THING.

AAIIEEEE!!

GRUUGH!
YEAGH!

SHIT!

BLAM!

EVERYONE OKAY?!
HUFF!
HUFF!
HUFF!

YOU KIDS NEED TO BE MORE CAREFUL--THESE THINGS SHOULDN'T BE ABLE TO SNEAK UP ON US.
ANDREA'S RIGHT, CARL. YOU NEED TO BE MORE CAREFUL.
LOOK!

EVERYONE IN THE TRUCK! WE'RE GETTING OUT OF HERE. THERE'S NO TELLING HOW MANY MORE OF THEM ARE IN THE WOODS.
HURRY!

WAIT--!
YOU HEARD YOUR DAD--C'MON!

YOU SHOULD GET IN THE TRUCK.
I CAN PROTECT MYSELF. DON'T WORRY ABOUT ME.

YOU GOT A PLAN?
LET'S MAKE SURE WE'RE NOT DEALING WITH ONLY TEN ROAMERS.
I DON'T WANT TO FLIP OUT AND DRIVE IN THE WRONG DIRECTION...

HELP!
HELP!
UNTIE ME, GOD DAMN IT!!

HOLD ON!

DON'T LET THEM GET CLOSE TO THE TRUCK!
BLAM!

BLAM!

YOU BETTER NOT BE A BAD GUY...

BLAM!

BLAM! BLAM! BLAM!

PKOW!

SHIT!

THE HEAD!
SHLOKK

BLAM!
HUUNGH.
PKOW!

GOD DAMN IT.

PKOW!

WE GOT IT COVERED OVER HERE, GUYS.

GLENN?

I GAVE HIM A GUN...
SORRY... WAS KIND OF IN THE MOMENT.

DID YOU HAVE TO GIVE HIM *THAT* GUN?

NOT TO WORRY, FRIEND.
I SEE NO REASON TO HOLD ONTO THIS THING. I TRUST YOU PEOPLE... AND I'M ONLY ASKING FOR THE TINIEST BIT OF TRUST BACK IN RETURN.
WHAT DO YOU SAY TO MY INVITATION?

WOW, AARON. YOU DON'T MISS A BEAT, DO YOU?
WHY ARE YOU IN SUCH A HURRY? THERE SOME KIND OF CUT-OFF FOR MEMBERSHIP IN YOUR LITTLE COMMUNITY?

MAYBE I JUST CARE MORE ABOUT YOUR FRIENDS THAN *YOU* DO?
ACTUALLY, LET ME APOLOGIZE FOR THAT NOW. COMMENTS LIKE THAT DON'T HELP ANYONE. FORGIVE MY SNARK.

IT'S LATE AND IT'S ONLY GETTING *LATER.* WE'VE GOT NO TIME TO SET UP CAMP AND WE'RE NOT IN A SAFE LOCATION AFTER THIS SHOOTOUT.
I'VE GOT A LOT OF PRESSING MATTERS TO DEAL WITH *RIGHT NOW.* I'M SURE YOU UNDERSTAND.

WE CAN SLEEP IN THE VEHICLES, KEEP A COUPLE MORE EXTRA PEOPLE UP FOR NIGHT WATCH TO BE SAFE.
WE SHOULD BE FINE.
YOU'RE WELCOME TO STAY WITH US OVERNIGHT. WE CAN DISCUSS THIS BUSINESS WITH YOU IN THE MORNING, AARON.

NO, FUCK THAT. I'M SORRY, BUT I'M GOING WITH HIM.
HE'S GOT A GROUP OF NEARLY FORTY PEOPLE WALLED IN A NEIGHBORHOOD AND HE'S INVITING US INTO IT.
AND FROM WHAT I CAN GATHER, ALL HE ASKS IN RETURN IS THAT WE PULL OUR OWN WEIGHT, CONTRIBUTE TO THE COMMUNITY... HELP IN WHATEVER WAY WE CAN.
WHAT IS THERE TO EVEN THINK ABOUT?
I KNOW YOU'RE SKEPTICAL, BUT THINK ABOUT IT. A COMMUNITY LIKE THAT WOULD NEED PEOPLE TO MAINTAIN IT. IT'S LIKE HE SAYS, HE NEEDS US AS MUCH AS WE NEED HIM.
RICK, I GET IT, YOU DON'T WANT TO RISK ANOTHER WOODBURY. I REMEMBER THE GOVERNOR, TRUST ME.
THIS MAN IS NOTHING LIKE HIM--I CAN TELL.
IF WE DON'T DO THIS--IF WE LET THIS PASS US BY--WHAT ARE WE DOING HERE? WHAT IS OUR PURPOSE?
DO WE JUST CONTINUE ON BEING MISERABLE, NEAR-STARVED AND DESPERATE? IS THAT OUR GOAL?
I THOUGHT THE WHOLE POINT OF THIS WAS TO FIND SOMETHING LIKE THIS--SOMETHING EXACTLY LIKE WHAT AARON IS OFFERING US.

I'M SORRY, BUT...
I DON'T CARE ABOUT ANYONE ELSE. NO MATTER WHAT YOU DECIDE... I, AT LEAST, AM GOING WITH HIM.

I'M WITH MICHONNE. I'M GOING, TOO.
ME TOO.
YEAH. I'M IN.
ROSITA?
SURE, WE'LL GIVE IT A SHOT.
WE COULD HAVE DISCUSSED THIS TOMORROW, EVERYONE. I WASN'T GOING TO STAND HERE AND DECIDE FOR EVERYONE.
I JUST THOUGHT THIS WAS SOMETHING WE NEEDED TO THINK ABOUT.
I DON'T NEED TO THINK ABOUT IT. I'M STARVING.
IF THERE'S FOOD, I'M THERE.
WELL, THAT'S MOST OF YOU.
GOOD.
DAD?
...
OKAY. IF THIS IS WHAT EVERYONE WANTS. OKAY.
AARON WILL STAY WITH US TONIGHT--WE'LL LEAVE FIRST THING IN THE MORNING.
LET'S GET SOME SLEEP.

HURRY, THEY'RE GOING TO LEAVE WITHOUT US.
LOOKS LIKE IT, DOESN'T IT? I GUESS ABRAHAM'S HUNGRIER THAN HE LET ON-- GETTING US ON THE ROAD AT THE CRACK OF DAWN...
THUNK!
YOU OKAY WITH THIS? YOU'RE THE ONLY ONE WHO NEVER SPOKE UP.
YOU WANT TO DO THIS?
DOESN'T MATTER NOW, DOES IT?
ANDREA, IF YOU HAVE A PROBLEM WITH THIS GUY, I'D LIKE TO KNOW THAT.
HE GIVE YOU A BAD FEELING?
THIS GUY? NO. AARON SEEMS LIKE A NICE ENOUGH GUY.
RICK, LISTEN...
WHEN AMY AND I WERE LIVING IN THE RV WITH DALE... BEFORE YOU EVEN MADE IT TO THE CAMP, I REALIZED MY PARENTS WERE PROBABLY DEAD. THAT WAS HARD...
...THEN I LOST AMY.

I FELT SO ALONE. IT DROVE ME INTO DALE'S ARMS AND I FELL IN LOVE WITH HIM.
THEN DONNA DIED... FOLLOWED BY ALLEN, AND DALE AND I WERE LEFT TO RAISE BEN AND BILLY.
I HAD A FAMILY... I'M TWENTY-SIX YEARS OLD... OVER THE COURSE OF A YEAR I INHERITED A FAMILY--I GREW UP--I LOVED THE WOMAN I BECAME AND THE LIFE I HAD.

AND NOW IT'S ALL GONE.
I'M ALL ALONE... AND ALL I CAN THINK ABOUT IS HOW I'M THAT GIRL AGAIN, THE GIRL I WAS... THE ONE I DIDN'T LIKE.

ALL I HAVE LEFT IS YOU... ALL OF YOU. YOU'RE THE ONLY THINGS LEFT TO REMIND ME OF WHAT I CAN BE.
THE ONLY THINGS KEEPING ME FROM BEING TRULY ALONE.

I'D FOLLOW YOU PEOPLE STRAIGHT INTO HELL.

LET'S HOPE THAT'S NOT WHAT YOU'RE DOING.

WHAT THE HELL? WHY ARE WE STOPPING SO SOON?

WHAT IS--?
OH, SHIT!

HANDS UP!
ANY SUDDEN MOVES AND I PUT ONE IN YOUR BRAIN, STRANGER!
TELL EVERYONE TO COME OUT OF THE WOODS NOW OR YOU DIE!

STOP! NO!
HE'S ALONE! HE'S WITH ME!
ARE YOU INSANE?
YOU COULDN'T TELL US ABOUT HIM BEFORE?

ANY MORE SURPRISES, AARON?

RICK, WE TALKED ABOUT TRUST. IT'S NOT EASY TO COME BY OUT HERE.
THIS IS MY PARTNER, ERIC. HE'S MY INSURANCE POLICY. I DIDN'T TELL YOU ABOUT HIM BECAUSE HE'S SUPPOSED TO KILL YOU AND SAVE ME IF YOU TURN OUT TO BE BAD PEOPLE.
YOU KNOCKED ME OUT--I LET IT SLIDE. I ONLY ASK FOR THE SAME CONSIDERATION HERE.

ONE MORE PERSON STEPS OUT OF THOSE WOODS AND I'M KILLING ***EVERYONE.***
THINK YOU MIGHT TELL US NOW IF ANYONE ELSE IS COMING OUT?

I PROMISE THIS IS IT. WE'RE A TWO-MAN OPERATION. WE MOVE FASTER THAT WAY. WE USUALLY SPOT THE GROUP FROM HIGH GROUND AND FOLLOW THEM AROUND.
THERE'S NO ONE ELSE OUT HERE. WE LISTENED TO YOU... I DECIDED THAT YOU WERE WORTH TALKING TO. I ALWAYS GO IN ALONE TO APPEAR LESS THREATENING.
WE OBSERVE FOR AS LONG AS WE CAN DEPENDING ON HOW FAST THE GROUP IS MOVING--THAT DICTATES HOW FAST WE HAVE TO MAKE A DECISION ON MAKING CONTACT OR NOT.

HOW LONG WERE YOU SPYING ON US?
HOW DID WE NEVER NOTICE YOU?
WE DIDN'T HAVE TO GET VERY CLOSE.
SOUND QUALITY'S NOT PERFECT, BUT THIS THING CAN PICK UP A CONVERSATION FROM ONE-HUNDRED YARDS AWAY.

LOAD ALL YOUR WEAPONS AND SUPPLIES INTO THE BACK OF OUR VAN. YOU GET THEM BACK WHEN WE ARRIVE AT YOUR PERFECT CAMP... SAFELY.
DEAL?

DEAL.

I KNOW WHAT THIS IS LIKE, I KNOW HOW UNCERTAIN YOU MUST FEEL. BUT I PROMISE YOU WON'T REGRET THIS.
YOU'LL EVENTUALLY LEARN... YOU CAN TRUST ME.
I WOULD LOVE FOR NOTHING ELSE THAN THAT TO BE TRUE.

EVERYONE PILE IN.
LET'S MOVE!

AARON.
YEAH?

NEXT TIME... NO MORE OVERNIGHTERS, OKAY?
MY NERVES CAN'T TAKE IT.
IT HAD TO BE DONE, ERIC. IT WAS HARD TO GET THESE PEOPLE TO TRUST ME. RUSHING THEM OUT IN THE MIDDLE OF THE NIGHT WOULD NOT HAVE WORKED.

THESE PEOPLE ARE GREAT.
THEY'RE TOUGH AS NAILS BUT GOOD AT HEART. WE *NEED* THESE PEOPLE.
ABRAHAM.
STOP.

I TRUST THIS GUY--AND THAT SCARES ME TO DEATH. I DON'T KNOW IF WE'RE DOING THE RIGHT THING HERE.
YOU GOT A READ ON HIM?
BEFORE EUGENE... I USED TO THINK I WAS PRETTY GOOD AT SPOTTING A LIAR. SEEMS LIKE HE'S ON THE LEVEL... BUT REALLY...
HOW CAN YOU EVER TELL?
WHAT I DO KNOW IS WE'RE RUNNING OUT OF FOOD AND HIS OFFER IS TOO GOOD TO PASS UP.

AGREED, BUT KEEP AN EYE ON HIM. ANY SURPRISE ALONG THE WAY... ANYTHING THAT DOESN'T SEEM RIGHT...
...SHOOT HIM IN THE HEAD.
WHEN SOMETHING SEEMS TOO GOOD TO BE TRUE...

...IT USUALLY *IS.*

I'LL WATCH OUT FOR ANYTHING SUSPICIOUS. WOULD BE ANYWAY, TO BE HONEST--NO MATTER HOW GOOD I FEEL ABOUT THESE GUYS.
THANKS.

WHAT WAS THAT ALL ABOUT?
JUST MAKING SURE EVERYONE IS ON THEIR TOES.

A SAFE COMMUNITY, LOADED WITH SUPPLIES, WELCOMING US IN WITH OPEN ARMS?
NO MATTER HOW HARD I TRY--I JUST CAN'T TAKE THAT AT FACE VALUE.

ARE YOU SURE YOU **EVER** WILL? I KNOW YOU... IT'LL BE SIX MONTHS FROM NOW AND YOU'LL STILL BE SLEEPING WITH ONE EYE OPEN.

YOU'RE PROBABLY RIGHT. WHAT IS **WRONG** WITH ME?
YOU'RE CAUTIOUS... IT MAKES YOU A GOOD LEADER-- IT'S HELPED US SURVIVE THIS LONG. DON'T FIGHT IT.
YOU CAN BE SKEPTICAL ALL YOU WANT-- BY ALL MEANS... BE **MISERABLE** AT THIS PLACE.
JUST DON'T RUIN IT FOR THE REST OF US.

BEEN TALKING TO HIM. HE SEEMS LIKE A REALLY COOL GUY. I HAVE TO BE HONEST HERE, RICK. I'M STARTING TO THINK WE'RE WORRYING FOR NOTHING.
LET'S HOPE SO. MADE GOOD TIME TODAY.
YEP.

SOUTH
Washington
NORTH
Gettysburg

THROK
ALL DONE! WE'VE GOT AS MUCH AS WE'RE GETTING!

OKAY, NEVER MIND... WE DON'T HAVE TO GO TO THIS PLACE NOW, DAD. I'M HAPPY OUT HERE.
A COUPLE TWINKIES A YEAR WILL KEEP ME HAPPY.

HOW DO YOU KNOW THEY DON'T HAVE THOSE THINGS BY THE CASE AT THIS PLACE WE'RE GOING?
OH! DO YOU THINK THEY MIGHT?!

OH, LOOK.
WE'RE GETTING CLOSE.

EXIT 7B
EXIT 7A
295 Balt-Wash Pkwy
LIGHT RAIL EXIT 6A
NORTH Baltimore EXIT 1/4 MILE
South Washington EXIT ONLY

RICK-- WAKE UP!

WE'RE STOPPING.

AARON! WHY ARE WE STOPPED?

THIS IS AS CLOSE AS WE'RE GOING TO COME TO THE CAPITAL--SAFER TO GO AROUND. SO I FIGURED WE'D STOP SO PEOPLE CAN TAKE A PEEK.

GRUH.

YOUR COMMUNITY IS RIGHT NEXT TO... THIS? ISN'T THAT DANGEROUS?

I ASSURE YOU, WE'VE TAKEN PRECAUTIONS. WE'RE COMPLETELY SAFE. YOU'LL SEE FOR YOURSELF, IN AN HOUR OR SO.
IT'S NOT FAR FROM HERE.

GOOD, WE--
FWEEEE!

WHAT IS IT?
A FLARE.

NO, GOD DAMN IT. WHAT DOES IT MEAN?

WE HAVE RUNNERS WHO COME INTO THE CITY FOR SUPPLIES. THEY HAVE FLARES.
THEY ONLY USE THEM IF THEY'RE SURROUNDED, TRAPPED OR HURT--

ERIC, DID YOU--?
I SAW IT. LET'S GO.

GUYS, I REALLY HATE TO BE A PRICK BUT I'M NOT LETTING **EITHER** OF YOU OUT OF MY SIGHT.
AARON, YOUR BUDDY STAYS HERE WITH THE GROUP--I'LL KEEP YOU COMPANY IF YOU'RE GOING DOWN THERE.

RICK, WITH ALL DUE RESPECT-- I REALLY WANT TO DO EVERYTHING IN MY POWER TO GET YOU TO TRUST ME-- BUT PEOPLE'S **LIVES** ARE AT STAKE.
WE JUST DON'T HAVE **TIME** FOR THIS.

WHAT'S GOING ON?
I'M GOING WITH AARON TO HELP HIM RESCUE SOMEONE. I NEED YOU TO WATCH CARL--WE SHOULD BE GONE FOR JUST A LITTLE WHILE.

ERIC WILL STAY HERE WITH THE REST, HE CAN MOVE THEM TO SAFER AREAS IF HE NEEDS TO.
I'M GOING AFTER MY PEOPLE.

IF YOU INSIST ON SOMEONE FROM YOUR GROUP COMING WITH ME, I'LL TAKE ABRAHAM.
WHAT IF I NEED TO CARRY SOMEONE?

CARRY?
WE'RE NOT GOING TO **WALK** DOWN THERE.

POLICE

TAKE THIS NEXT RIGHT, ABRAHAM.
WE'RE GETTING CLOSE--SO SLOW IT UP A LITTLE.

THIS DOESN'T LOOK GOOD.
THERE'S TOO DAMN MANY.

WHEN WE DO STOP--WE NEED TO MAKE IT QUICK.
THE ONES YOU SEE ARE ONLY THE TIP OF THE ICEBERG-- TRUST ME.

HEY-- WHAT IS--?
THAT'S THEM!
STOP THE VAN!

JESUS!

HELP ME KEEP AN EYE ON THE AREA--THIS COULD GET REAL UGLY, REAL QUICK.
AGREED.

JESUS CHRIST, HEATH--WHAT *HAPPENED* TO HIM?
HE TRIED JUMPING TO THE NEXT BUILDING--DIDN'T MAKE IT. FELL JUST THE RIGHT WAY...

...BROKE HIS LEG. HE'S BEEN ON THE VERGE OF PASSING OUT EVER SINCE.

WAS ABLE TO POP OFF THE FLARE--BEEN TRYING TO KEEP THEM BACK. GLAD YOU WERE IN THE AREA, MAN.
BUT, UH--WHO ARE THESE GUYS?

THIS IS RICK AND ABRAHAM.
THEY'RE WITH ME, NEW CITIZENS. WE WERE ON OUR WAY BACK WHEN WE SAW THE FLARE.

WHAT CHANCE DOES THIS GUY HAVE? LOOK AT THAT. IT'S GOING TO GET INFECTED-- AND *THEN* WHAT?
YOU HAVE SOMEONE WHO CAN FIX *THAT?*
NICE FRIENDS YOU'RE MAKING, AARON.
NO OFFENSE, BUT THIS GUY HAS *DAVIDSON* WRITTEN ALL OVER HIM.
IGNORE HIM, RICK.
THINGS ARE GOING TO BE DIFFERENT NOW. WE HAVE THREE DOCTORS IN OUR COMMUNITY. ONE OF THEM IS A SURGEON.

GET HIM IN THE VAN!
WE NEED TO GET THE FUCK OUT OF HERE RIGHT FUCKING NOW!
RATATATAT!

BRAKK! BRAKK! BRAKK!

GET THE DOORS OPEN!
BRAKK! BRAKK!

HURRY!
HURRY!

I'LL STAY WITH SCOTT. HEATH, YOU AND ABRAHAM DRIVE THE BIKES BACK. YOU LEAD THE WAY. WE'LL FOLLOW.

I'M STAYING IN THE BACK, MAKE SURE THIS GUY'S OKAY.
RICK, CAN YOU DRIVE THE VAN?

BRAKK! BRAKK! BRAKK!
NICE TO MEET YOU.
I'M RESERVING JUDGMENT ON THAT UNTIL LATER.

FUCK!
FUCK!
FUCK!
SKRUNGG!
FUCK.

GRAARRGH.

BRAKKA! BRAKKA! BRAK
BRAKKA! BRAKKA! BRAK
RAKKA! BRAKKA! BRAKKA!

HOLY SHIT, AM I GLAD TO SEE YOU GUYS!
THEY'RE WITH YOU?
WHEW.

SO THESE ARE YOUR PEOPLE?
TRUST ME, RICK--I'D BE THE FIRST TO YELL TURN AROUND IF THEY WEREN'T. THESE ARE THE GUYS THAT'LL BE KEEPING YOU AND YOUR PEOPLE SAFE FROM NOW ON.
THEY'RE GOOD PEOPLE.

WE'VE CLEARED A PATH--GET MOVING BEFORE THE GAP CLOSES UP! WE'LL FOLLOW YOU OUT--KEEPING THEM OFF YOU.
COME ON!
MOVE!

BRAKKA! BRAKKA! BRAKKA!

HEH...
WHAT IS IT?
I'D ALWAYS WANTED TO COME HERE...

WHAT'S *TAKING* THEM SO LONG...?

I KNOW YOU'RE WORRIED. YOUR DAD KNOWS WHAT HE'S DOING, CARL.
HE'S BARELY BEEN GONE TWO HOURS.

OH, LOOK AT THAT.

IT WENT FINE. GUY'S GOT SOME KIND OF FUCKED UP LEG.
THIS TRUCK FULL OF GUNMEN CAME AND SAVED US. THE TIME TO BACK OUT OF JOINING THESE PEOPLE HAS PASSED... NO TURNING BACK NOW.
STILL FINE WITH ME.

SCOTT'S LEG IS BUSTED REAL BAD. WE'VE GOTTA GET HIM BACK TO THE COMMUNITY.
GATHER UP THESE PEOPLE-- LET'S GO.
OKAY. I'LL LET THEM ALL KNOW.

I'M RIDING WITH YOU GUYS. IT'S COLD IN THE BACK OF THAT TRUCK.
CLIMB ON IN.

OKAY, WE'VE GOT AN INJURED MAN WHO NEEDS HELP. LET'S MOVE!

HOW CLOSE ARE WE?
VERY. WON'T BE AN HOUR.

Alexandria

THIS IS IT. IT'LL TAKE THEM A SECOND TO OPEN THE GATE.
THERE'S A PARKING AREA TO THE RIGHT ONCE WE'RE IN. SOMEONE SHOULD COME OUT TO GREET US...
RICK... YOU MADE IT.
...

WHOA--
DAD, ARE
YOU SEEING
THIS?!

DAD?

OVER HERE TO THE RIGHT.
PARK THERE.

LET ME GO TELL THEM YOU'RE HERE. IT'LL TAKE A MINUTE FOR ME TO EXPLAIN.
DOUGLAS AND THE OTHERS-- THEY'LL WANT TO TALK TO YOU AND YOUR PEOPLE. IT'S PART OF THE PROCESS.
I'LL COME GET YOU WHEN THEY'RE READY.

THEY'RE GOING TO TALK TO US... THEN WE'RE FREE TO ENTER.
THEY'RE GOING TO INTERVIEW ALL OF US? THAT'S GOING TO TAKE FOREVER.
THIS IS FUCKING WEIRD.

EVERYTHING IS GOING TO BE DIFFERENT NOW.

CARL WILL BE ABLE TO MAKE A LOT OF NEW FRIENDS. THERE ARE MANY FAMILIES HERE.
I CAN SEE THAT... IT'S, THIS ISN'T SOMETHING WE'VE SEEN IN A VERY LONG TIME. IT'S NOT SOMETHING I THOUGHT I'D EVER SEE AGAIN.

HAPPY CHILDREN.

YES, WELL... I THINK YOU'LL FIND, FOR THE MOST PART, WE ARE ABLE TO RETURN TO THE LIFE WE REMEMBER WITHIN THESE WALLS.
DOUGLAS IS READY TO SEE YOU.

DOUGLAS?
HE'S OUR... FOR LACK OF A BETTER WORD, LEADER. HE'S WHO WE LOOK TO FOR GUIDANCE. HE MAKES SURE EVERYONE IS DOING THEIR JOB, PULLING THEIR WEIGHT.
MY WORD CARRIES A LOT OF WEIGHT, BUT HE STILL WANTS TO TALK TO YOU.

ANSWER ALL HIS QUESTIONS HONESTLY, EVEN IF YOU FEEL LIKE YOU SHOULDN'T, AND YOU'LL BE FINE.
IT'S THAT HOUSE THERE. HE'S WAITING FOR YOU.
OKAY.

HELLO?
DIDN'T KNOW IF I SHOULD JUST COME IN.

DOUGLAS?

I KNOW, RIGHT?
WEIRD BEING IN A HOUSE AFTER ALL THIS TIME. ONE THAT ISN'T RAVAGED-- OR LOOTED...
OR BURNT.

I'M DOUGLAS... DOUGLAS MONROE.
IT'S GOOD TO MEET YOU.

RICK GRIMES.
AARON SAYS GOOD THINGS ABOUT YOU AND YOUR PEOPLE, RICK.

I'LL HAVE TO THANK HIM FOR THAT. I ASSURE YOU THEY'RE ALL TRUE--IF THAT'S WHAT I'M HERE FOR.
WHAT EXACTLY AM I HERE FOR?

TO TALK.
THAT'S ALL.

PLEASE, HAVE A SEAT.

MAKE NO MISTAKE, THE MAJORITY OF WHAT DECIDES WHETHER OR NOT YOU LIVE HERE-- IS WHAT AARON AND ERIC SEE BEFORE THEY EVEN CONTACT YOU.
THE IDEA IS TO OBSERVE HOW YOU ACT WHEN YOU THINK YOU'RE NOT BEING WATCHED. THEY'RE LOOKING FOR RED FLAGS.
ARE YOU TRAVELING WITH WOMEN AND CHILDREN? IF SO, HOW ARE THEY TREATED? ARE YOU LOOKING FOR FOOD OR DRUGS? HOW DO YOU TREAT EACH OTHER? SIMPLE THINGS--BUT EASY TO SPOT.
IT'S ASTONISHINGLY EASY TO GET A READ ON PEOPLE BY WATCHING THEM LIKE AARON DOES.
THE THINGS HE'S SEEN...
NOW, MYSELF... IF YOU WATCHED C-SPAN RELIGIOUSLY YOU MIGHT EVEN KNOW WHO I AM.
CONGRESSMAN DOUGLAS MONROE, DEMOCRATIC REPRESENTATIVE FROM THE SECOND DISTRICT OF OHIO.
DIDN'T LOOK LIKE THIS, THOUGH. I CAN'T STAND HAVING DIRTY HAIR. COULDN'T WASH IT... SO I CUT IT ALL OFF.
THE GOATEE IS SOMETHING I'D ALWAYS WANTED TO TRY, BUT WAS FROWNED UPON POLITICALLY.
THESE DAYS, I FIND NO EXCUSE NOT TO INDULGE MYSELF.
I SHOULD WARN YOU, I AM KNOWN TO RAMBLE. I DON'T MEAN TO BORE YOU, BUT POLITICIANS LIKE TO TALK.
I FEEL IT'S IMPORTANT WE GET TO KNOW EACH OTHER.
I FEEL THE SAME WAY. CARRY ON.
IF YOU SAID LESS, I'D WANT TO ASK YOU QUESTIONS. IF I'M GOING TO LIVE HERE--I WANT TO KNOW EVERYTHING I CAN ABOUT MOST EVERYONE HERE.
GOOD ANSWER, YOU SHOULD WANT TO KNOW EVERYTHING ABOUT US.
AARON WAS RIGHT ABOUT YOU. SMART MAN.
THIS COMMUNITY HAS EXISTED FOR LESS THAN A YEAR. I LIVED IN THE OPEN FOR THREE MONTHS.
DURING THAT TIME I KILLED TWO MEN. NOT WALKERS, MIND YOU... ACTUAL LIVING MEN.
YOU DO NOT SEEM THE LEAST BIT APPREHENSIVE TO LEARN THAT I'VE KILLED PEOPLE.
I ASSUME IT NEEDED TO BE DONE.
IT ABSOLUTELY DID.

I WANT TO TELL YOU A STORY.
BEFORE THIS WORLD SPIRALED INTO CHAOS, BEFORE THE DEAD STARTED WALKING, I READ A NEWS ARTICLE ON THE INTERNET. IT'S THE KIND OF THING I USUALLY TRY TO AVOID.
BEING A FATHER, I HATE STORIES OF KIDS GETTING HURT, IT REALLY TEARS ME UP. BUT YOU KNOW HOW IT IS--YOU CAN'T NOT LISTEN WHEN THE NEWS STARTS--AND AFTER YOU HAVE KIDS, THOSE STORIES SPRING OUT OF THE WHITE NOISE--YOU CAN'T HELP BUT HEAR THEM.
THE PARENTS WHO SHAKE THEIR KIDS. THE CHILDREN LEFT IN THE CAR ON A HOT SUMMER DAY. BABIES LEFT IN TRASH CANS--IT'S ***HORRIBLE.***
BUT THIS ONE, THE ONE I SAW ON THE INTERNET... IT STILL HAUNTS ME, EVEN TODAY.
A MAN IN FLORIDA, FORT LAUDERDALE IF I RECALL CORRECTLY, WAS ON A DRUG OF SOME KIND. I DON'T REMEMBER WHICH-- SOME TYPE OF HALLUCINOGEN, I WOULD ASSUME.
WHILE UNDER THE INFLUENCE OF THESE DRUGS... HE-- HE ***ATE*** HIS FOUR YEAR OLD SON'S EYEBALLS.
JUST ATE THEM RIGHT OUT OF HIS HEAD.
ASIDE FROM THE STORY IN GENERAL BEING JUST... ***HORRIFIC,*** THE THING THAT REALLY STUCK WITH ME, THAT SENDS SHIVERS DOWN MY SPINE TO THIS VERY DAY... WAS A QUOTE FROM THE SON.

"DADDY ATE MY EYES."

NO ANGER, NO FEAR... JUST *"DADDY ATE MY EYES."*
HE SAYS IT AS IF HE BELIEVES IT'S SOMETHING NORMAL, THAT HAPPENS TO ***EVERYONE.***
FOUR YEARS OLD. THE POOR BOY DOESN'T KNOW ANY DIFFERENT.

TALKING ABOUT IT NOW, IT STILL MAKES ME UNCOMFORTABLE. THE DAY I READ THE STORY... I WAS WRECKED. I ACCOMPLISHED VERY LITTLE THAT DAY.
I JUST COULDN'T STOP THINKING ABOUT THAT STORY, ABOUT THAT POOR LITTLE BOY.
I CAN'T STOP MYSELF FROM FILLING IN THE BLANKS OF THE STORY...
...THE DETAILS NOT TOLD BUT IMPLIED.
I PICTURE THE FATHER, PLACING HIS HANDS ON EITHER SIDE OF HIS SON'S HEAD--I THINK ABOUT WHAT WOULD BE GOING THROUGH THAT BOY'S MIND AT THE TIME.
HE WOULDN'T BE SCARED, THIS IS HIS DAD, HE WOULD HAVE NO CLUE WHAT TO EXPECT. THIS WAS HIS FATHER FOR CHRIST'S SAKE--HE WOULDN'T IMMEDIATELY ASSUME THIS MAN WAS GOING TO HURT HIM.
THE MECHANICS OF IT STILL HAUNT ME. IS IT EASY TO JUST SUCK A PERSON'S EYEBALLS RIGHT OUT OF THEIR HEAD? CAN IT BE DONE QUICKLY? HOW MUCH TIME PASSED BETWEEN THE REMOVAL OF EACH EYE?
ALL QUESTIONS I DESPERATELY DO NOT WANT TO KNOW THE ANSWER TO, BUT CAN'T STOP MYSELF FROM ASKING.

CHILDREN... THEY'RE HELPLESS... THEY CAN'T DEFEND THEMSELVES. THEY RELY ON US FOR THAT, THEIR PARENTS. THAT'S WHAT WE'RE THERE FOR.
HURTING YOUR OWN CHILD... IT'S SUCH A BETRAYAL. THIS BOY IS BLIND NOW, HIS LIFE IS FOREVER CHANGED-- BECAUSE OF HIS ASSHOLE FATHER.
THIS INSANE PRICK WHO SHOULD NEVER HAVE HAD A CHILD-- I THINK ABOUT WHAT HE'S DONE TO THIS CHILD...
...EVEN THEN, BEFORE ALL THIS-- I THOUGHT ABOUT WHAT THIS MONSTER HAD DONE TO HIS OWN FLESH AND BLOOD, AND THOUGHT TO MYSELF...
...IF I COULD GET AWAY WITH IT, I WOULD KILL THIS MAN FOR WHAT HE'S DONE.

I DON'T TELL THAT STORY TO OFFEND YOU, I KNOW YOU HAVE A YOUNG SON.
THE POINT IS THAT THERE IS EVIL IN THE WORLD... ALWAYS WAS, LONG BEFORE IT CAME IN THE UNDEAD VARIETY.

IF ANYTHING... THINGS ONLY GOT WORSE AFTER THE COLLAPSE. PEOPLE WHO WERE KEEPING THEMSELVES IN CHECK, LIVING BY SOCIETY'S RULES... THEY NO LONGER HAD ANY CHECKS AND BALANCES.
THE CRAZY, FREE TO ROAM, UNCHECKED-- A WORLD GONE MAD.

AND SOMEHOW... YOU AND YOUR PEOPLE SURVIVED OUT THERE FOR HOW LONG?
FOURTEEN MONTHS, BY OUR COUNT. OUR CALENDAR COULD BE A BIT INACCURATE.
REMARKABLE.

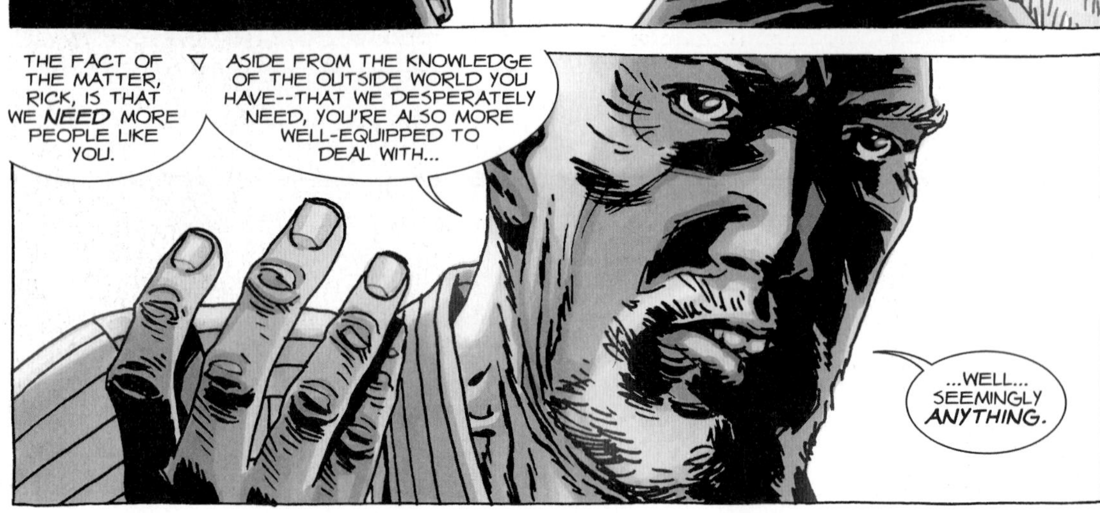

THE FACT OF THE MATTER, RICK, IS THAT WE NEED MORE PEOPLE LIKE YOU.
ASIDE FROM THE KNOWLEDGE OF THE OUTSIDE WORLD YOU HAVE--THAT WE DESPERATELY NEED, YOU'RE ALSO MORE WELL-EQUIPPED TO DEAL WITH...
...WELL... SEEMINGLY ANYTHING.

WHAT DO YOU WANT ME TO SAY?

I WANT YOU TO TELL ME WHAT YOU DID FOR A LIVING BEFORE ALL THIS.
THAT'S SOMETHING I DON'T KNOW. IT HELPS US DECIDE WHAT YOU'D BE BEST FOR HERE IN THE COMMUNITY, HOW YOU'D BE OF BEST USE.

I WAS A POLICE OFFICER.

WELL, THAT CINCHES IT. I WAS ALREADY THINKING ALONG THESE LINES BUT YEAH, THAT'S MADE UP MY MIND.
YOU'RE OUR CONSTABLE.
CONSTABLE?

I ALWAYS PREFERRED THAT WORD TO ALL THE OTHERS. POLICE OFFICER, COP... YOU ARE WHAT YOU WERE BEFORE. IT'S PERFECT.
ADDING YOUR GROUP TO THE MIX, I BELIEVE THAT WILL PUT US OVER SIXTY. WITH THAT MANY PEOPLE HERE, THERE'S BOUND TO BE AN OCCASIONAL PROBLEM TO DEAL WITH. PEOPLE FIGHT--IT'S IN OUR NATURE.
WE NEED SOMEONE WITH AUTHORITY.

THAT'S HOW IT WORKS? YOU SAY WHAT WE DO AND WE DO IT?

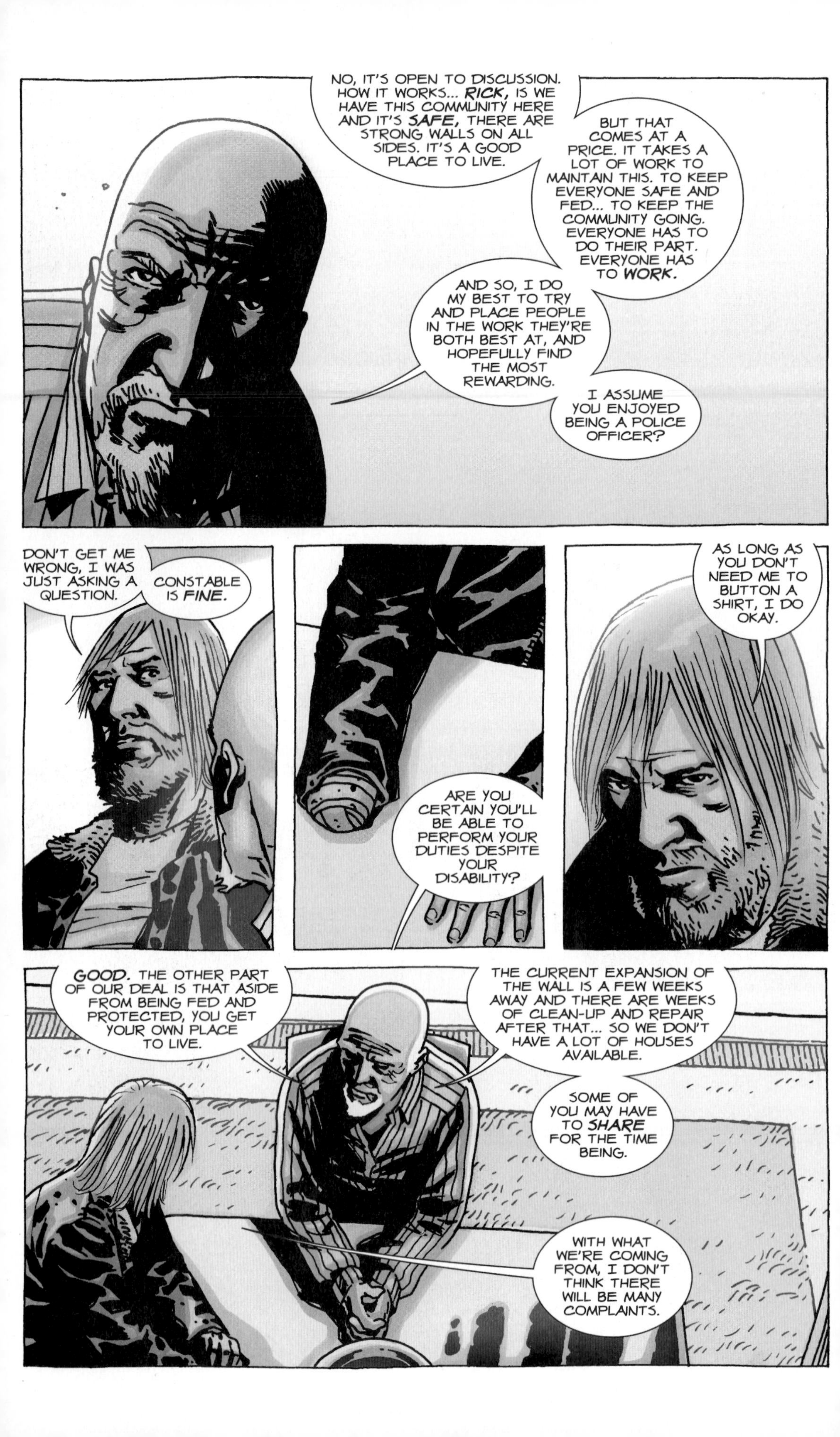
NO, IT'S OPEN TO DISCUSSION. HOW IT WORKS... RICK, IS WE HAVE THIS COMMUNITY HERE AND IT'S SAFE, THERE ARE STRONG WALLS ON ALL SIDES. IT'S A GOOD PLACE TO LIVE.
BUT THAT COMES AT A PRICE. IT TAKES A LOT OF WORK TO MAINTAIN THIS. TO KEEP EVERYONE SAFE AND FED... TO KEEP THE COMMUNITY GOING. EVERYONE HAS TO DO THEIR PART. EVERYONE HAS TO WORK.
AND SO, I DO MY BEST TO TRY AND PLACE PEOPLE IN THE WORK THEY'RE BOTH BEST AT, AND HOPEFULLY FIND THE MOST REWARDING.
I ASSUME YOU ENJOYED BEING A POLICE OFFICER?
DON'T GET ME WRONG, I WAS JUST ASKING A QUESTION.
CONSTABLE IS FINE.
ARE YOU CERTAIN YOU'LL BE ABLE TO PERFORM YOUR DUTIES DESPITE YOUR DISABILITY?
AS LONG AS YOU DON'T NEED ME TO BUTTON A SHIRT, I DO OKAY.
GOOD. THE OTHER PART OF OUR DEAL IS THAT ASIDE FROM BEING FED AND PROTECTED, YOU GET YOUR OWN PLACE TO LIVE.
THE CURRENT EXPANSION OF THE WALL IS A FEW WEEKS AWAY AND THERE ARE WEEKS OF CLEAN-UP AND REPAIR AFTER THAT... SO WE DON'T HAVE A LOT OF HOUSES AVAILABLE.
SOME OF YOU MAY HAVE TO SHARE FOR THE TIME BEING.
WITH WHAT WE'RE COMING FROM, I DON'T THINK THERE WILL BE MANY COMPLAINTS.

EXCELLENT. WELL, RICK... THAT WILL BE ALL.
WE'RE DONE.

NOW, THERE WILL BE A TOUR, AND SOME KIND OF MEET AND GREET AROUND DINNER TIME. AND HOME ASSIGNMENT. YOU AND YOUR PEOPLE HAVE A BIG DAY AHEAD OF YOU.
I'D LIKE TO TALK TO A FEW MORE OF THEM TODAY AS TIME PERMITS.

THAT ALL SOUNDS FINE, DOUGLAS.

WELCOME TO OUR COMMUNITY.
THANK YOU FOR HAVING US.

TOLD YOU IT'D BE NO BIG DEAL.

YEAH, SEEMS LIKE A NICE ENOUGH GUY. HE WANTS ME TO SEND SOMEONE ELSE IN THERE TO TALK.
ANDREA? YOU WANT TO GO?
SURE.

HOUSE ACROSS THE STREET HERE HAS OPENED UP TO NEW ARRIVALS. SOME OF YOUR FRIENDS ARE IN THERE TAKING SHOWERS.
MIGHT WANT TO GET IN ON THAT BEFORE THE HOT WATER RUNS OUT.
WHERE'S CARL?

WHERE'S MY SON?!
WHOA, RICK-- CALM DOWN.

HE'S PLAYING WITH THE OTHER KIDS. SOPHIA, TOO.
THEY'RE OKAY.

OH, OKAY.

DID YOU SAY SOMETHING ABOUT A WORKING SHOWER?

PLEASE, HAVE A SEAT. MY NAME IS DOUGLAS MONROE. IT'S GOOD TO MEET YOU...
ANDREA.
IT'S GOOD TO MEET YOU ANDREA.

SO, WHAT WAS IT YOU DID BEFORE? WHAT KIND OF JOB DID YOU HAVE?

I WAS A FILE CLERK AT A LAWYER'S OFFICE. BUT I'M NOT NEARLY AS USELESS AS THAT WOULD MAKE ME SOUND.
I'M REALLY GOOD WITH A GUN.

REALLY?
HOW GOOD?
VERY GODDAMN GOOD.
IT'S KIND OF RIDICULOUS.

ARE YOU SINGLE?

EXCUSE ME?

OH, I'M SORRY. DON'T MISUNDERSTAND. THAT'S SOMETHING I'M ASKING EVERYONE. IT HELPS US PLAN THE HOUSING.
SO?

WOW.

I WILL NEVER GET USED TO THIS.

KNOCK! KNOCK!
JUST A MINUTE.

I'M SORRY TO BOTHER YOU, BUT DOUGLAS WANTED ME TO SEE IF THIS FITS.
WOW, HE DOESN'T WASTE ANY TIME.

YOU KNOW, I CAN CUT HAIR.

HOW IS ALL THIS POSSIBLE? WHO STARTED THIS?
A MAN NAMED DAVIDSON STARTED BUILDING THE FENCE. DOUGLAS CAME LATER. ALL BEFORE MY TIME. I'M OLIVIA, IF YOU WERE WONDERING.
THE AREA IS RUN ON AN ISOLATED SOLAR POWER GRID. IT WAS PUT TOGETHER BY THE GOVERNMENT IN CASE SOMETHING LIKE THIS HAPPENED.

REALLY? THAT'S AMAZING.

NOT REALLY. IT DOESN'T WORK AT ALL THE WAY IT WAS SUPPOSED TO. HALF THE HOUSES HERE CAN'T GET HOT WATER AND WE DON'T HAVE ENOUGH POWER TO RUN LIGHTS ALL THE TIME.
HENCE THE DARKNESS.

IT'S NOT PERFECT, SURE... BUT COMING FROM HOW WE'VE BEEN LIVING, THIS IS GREAT.

SURE, HONEY. I GIVE YOU TWO WEEKS BEFORE YOU'RE COMPLAINING ABOUT A READING LAMP NOT WORKING AT NIGHT.
JUST YOU WATCH.

WHOA, WOULD YOU LOOK AT THAT? YOU CLEAN UP REAL NICE, RICK.
LIKE A NEW MAN. I HARDLY RECOGNIZE YOU.
HANDSOME.
HARDLY RECOGNIZE MYSELF.
WHERE IS EVERYONE?
ROSITA IS INSIDE TALKING TO DOUGLAS, SEEMS LIKE A NICE GUY.
SAYS I'D BE BEST ON THEIR CONSTRUCTION CREW, BUILDING NEW WALLS AND WHATNOT, THEY ALSO PROTECT THE PERIMETER. ON ACCOUNT OF MY MILITARY BACKGROUND.
THEY'RE GOING TO ROUND US UP IN A FEW MINUTES FOR SOME KIND OF TOUR, THEN THEY'RE GOING TO ASSIGN US PLACES TO STAY FOR THE NIGHT.
LET ME GO CHECK ON CARL.
HEY, GUYS-- EVERYTHING OKAY HERE?
EVERYTHING IS GREAT! THIS PLACE IS GREAT, DAD!

HEY, FELLA. I'M CARL'S DAD. YOU MIND ME ASKING WHAT HAPPENED TO YOUR EYE?
UH...

BALL HIT ME IN THE FACE YESTERDAY, WAS MY OWN FAULT.
LOOKS BAD, HUH?

LOOKS LIKE A BLACK EYE.
DON'T WORRY, IT MAKES YOU LOOK TOUGH.

I'LL LET YOU BOYS GET BACK TO YOUR GAME.
HAVE FUN, CARL.
I WILL, DAD.

EXCUSE ME.

WHO WAS THAT?
DOUGLAS'S WIFE, REGINA... AND SHE'S NOT HAPPY ABOUT SOMETHING.

DOUGLAS!
WHAT THE HELL ARE YOU DOING?!

WHAT IS IT NOW, REGINA?
SORRY, HEATH.

WHAT IS IT NOW?! I'LL TELL YOU WHAT IT IS--WHO THE HELL ARE THESE PEOPLE AND WHY HAVE YOU LET THEM INSIDE?!
YOU'RE PUTTING US ALL IN DANGER!

PLEASE CALM DOWN. I'M NOT GOING TO TALK TO YOU IF WE'RE JUST GOING TO YELL.
UNDERSTOOD?

TELL ME EVERYTHING YOU KNOW ABOUT THESE PEOPLE.
NOW.

I UNDERSTAND THAT YOU'RE CONCERNED, BUT YOU KNOW HOW IT IS, WE NEED THESE PEOPLE TO KEEP OUR COMMUNITY GROWING. THAT'S HOW WE'VE BEEN ABLE TO LAST THIS LONG.
I'LL ADMIT, AT FIRST GLANCE THEY ALL SEEM LIKE GOOD PEOPLE TO ME.
ONLY ONE HAS ME SUSPICIOUS IS RICK, THEIR LEADER.
TRUST ME, HE'S ON THE LEVEL. WE NEED HIM HERE MORE THAN ANYONE.
WHAT COULD WE POSSIBLY NEED HIM FOR? JUST LOOK AT HIM!

WE NEED HIM BECAUSE HE'S SURVIVED OUT IN THE OPEN MORE THAN ANYONE ELSE HERE. MOST EVERYONE IN HIS GROUP HAS.
HE KNOWS WHAT IT TAKES TO SURVIVE--AND WE'RE GOING TO LEARN FROM HIM. HE'S GOING TO BE ABLE TO THINK OF THINGS WE'D NEVER CONSIDER.
THIS NEW GUY IS GOING TO BE OUR SALVATION, JUST YOU WATCH.

OR HE MAY JUST TURN OUT TO BE ANOTHER DAVIDSON.

DAVIDSON?!

WHAT HAVE I TOLD YOU?! I DON'T EVER WANT TO HEAR THE MAN'S NAME AGAIN!
EVER!
NOT AFTER WHAT HE DID.

NOT AFTER WHAT HE MADE US DO.

DOUGLAS.
SERIOUSLY, MAN. WHAT THE HELL?

I KNOW. I'M SORRY.
YOU KNOW HOW I FEEL, YOU KNOW WHAT I'VE SAID. I DIDN'T MEAN TO OVERREACT.

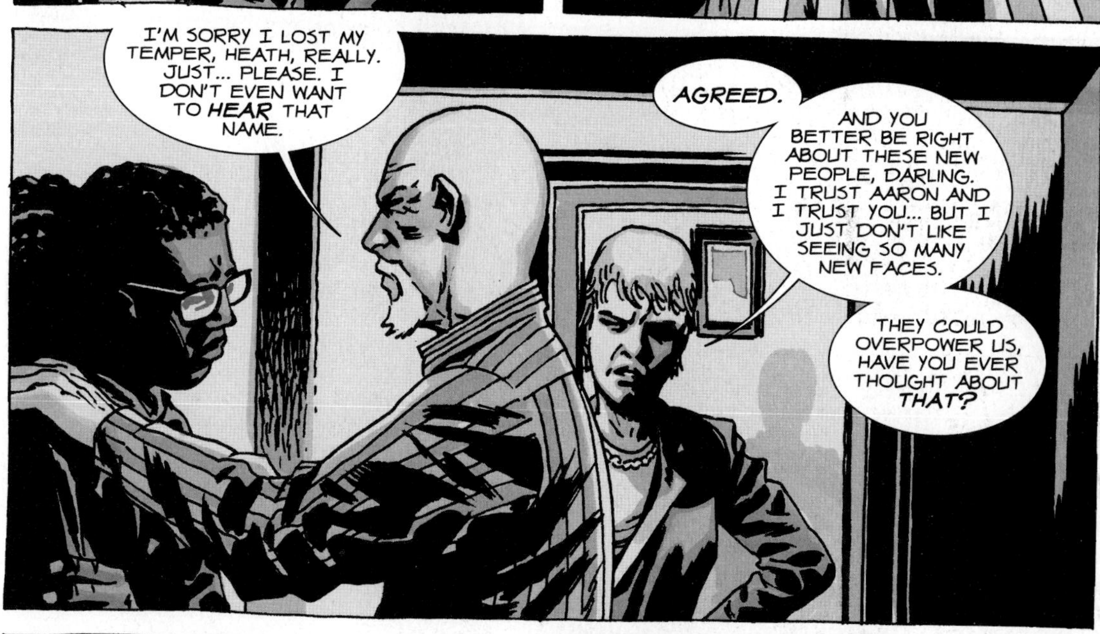
I'M SORRY I LOST MY TEMPER, HEATH, REALLY. JUST... PLEASE. I DON'T EVEN WANT TO HEAR THAT NAME.
AGREED.
AND YOU BETTER BE RIGHT ABOUT THESE NEW PEOPLE, DARLING. I TRUST AARON AND I TRUST YOU... BUT I JUST DON'T LIKE SEEING SO MANY NEW FACES.
THEY COULD OVERPOWER US, HAVE YOU EVER THOUGHT ABOUT THAT?

REGINA, DEAR-- WITH ALL DUE RESPECT, CALM DOWN. WE'VE THROWN THESE PEOPLE A LIFE RAFT. THEY'RE HAPPY TO BE HERE.
JUST THE SAME, EVERYONE HERE WILL KEEP AN EYE OUT FOR ANYTHING WEIRD OR OFF IN ANY WAY.

NOW IF YOU'LL EXCUSE ME. I'M GOING TO GIVE OUR NEW FRIENDS A QUICK TOUR AROUND THE COMMUNITY.

I'M GETTING MY *DAD!*
FINE. DO IT!
CARL-- WHAT'S GOING ON?!

HE WANTED TO SEE MY GUN. I TOLD HIM NO AND HE PUSHED ME.
SO I PUSHED HIM BACK.

CARL, YOU...
YOU SHOULDN'T BE LETTING ANYONE HOLD YOUR GUN, BUT YOU SHOULDN'T BE PUSHING--

LISTEN, I KNOW YOU WERE JUST DEFENDING YOURSELF, BUT I DON'T WANT YOU TO HURT THESE KIDS.
UNDERSTAND?
YEAH.

I'M SORRY I KNOCKED YOU DOWN.
UNGH.

DON'T TOUCH ME.
I'M TELLING MY *DAD.*

EVERYONE OKAY?
BOYS BEING BOYS...
I UNDERSTAND THAT ALL TOO WELL.
LOOKS LIKE YOU'VE SETTLED IN NICELY.
AND IN RECORD TIME.
YEAH... FEELS WEIRD, TOO.
THIS IS GOING TO TAKE SOME GETTING USED TO. FACE FEELS COLD.
WELL, I'M GOING TO HAVE TO PUT A HOLD ON THE SHOWERS FOR NOW. GATHER UP ALL YOUR PEOPLE. I WANT TO TAKE THEM ON A QUICK WALK THROUGH THE GROUNDS.
I'D LIKE TO GET YOU GUYS SETTLED INTO SOME HOUSES BEFORE DARK.
WILL DO.

OH, AND WE'LL NEED TO TAKE ALL YOUR WEAPONS. WE DON'T ALLOW THOSE INSIDE THE WALLS.

WHICH ONE IS IT?
THAT ONE THERE.

HEY, *YOU*-- COME HERE, LITTLE BOY!
WHOA, CALM DOWN THERE, MISTER.

GET YOUR HANDS OFF ME, PAL.
THAT *YOUR* SON? THE ONE IN THE COWBOY HAT?
IT IS.

YOU AWARE YOUR SON IS PICKING ON MY BOY?
WITH ALL DUE RESPECT, I DON'T BELIEVE THAT'S WHAT ACTUALLY HAPPENED.
YOU KNOW HOW IT IS, BOYS WILL BE BOYS. YOUR SON ASKED TO SEE MY SON'S GUN, WHEN HE REFUSED, YOUR SON PUSHED HIM AND MINE PUSHED BACK.

YOUR SON HAS A *GUN?*

WHAT THE HELL IS GOING ON HERE, DOUGLAS?
WE'RE TAKING THEIR WEAPONS NOW. WE DIDN'T KNOW THE BOY WAS CARRYING A GUN, TOO.

WE'RE STILL SETTLING IN. WE'VE ONLY BEEN HERE FOR A FEW HOURS...
I'M SORRY, I DON'T BELIEVE I CAUGHT YOUR NAME.
IT'S *NICHOLAS.* THIS IS MY SON MIKEY.

WELL, NICHOLAS. I'M RICK. DOUGLAS HAS ASKED ME TO KEEP AN EYE ON THINGS AROUND THE COMMUNITY. I'LL BE KEEPING THE PEACE.
I CERTAINLY UNDERSTAND YOUR ANGER. WERE THE ROLES REVERSED, I COULD EASILY SEE MYSELF BEHAVING THE SAME WAY.
THING IS, I WOULDN'T WANT SOME UNKNOWN KID SHOWING MY SON A GUN EITHER.

ABSOLUTELY *NOT.*

SO WE'VE GOTTEN TO THE BOTTOM OF THIS LITTLE MISUNDERSTANDING. GOOD.
YOU SEEM LIKE A NICE GUY, NICHOLAS. I'M SURE MY SON AND YOURS WILL GET ALONG REAL WELL... ONCE HE STOPS PACKING HEAT.

GOOD, IF EVERYONE WILL PLEASE FOLLOW ME. WE'LL DROP YOUR WEAPONS OFF AND GET STARTED ON YOUR TOUR.
NICHOLAS, YOU'RE WELCOME TO JOIN US IF YOU'D LIKE.
NO THANKS, DOUGLAS. I'VE SEEN THE PLACE BEFORE.

THIS HOUSE ALSO ACTS AS OUR ARMORY, FOR ALL INTENTS AND PURPOSES. WE KEEP ALL OUR WEAPONS HERE, CLOSEST TO THE GATE. FOR SAFETY PURPOSES WE DO NOT ALLOW ANY WEAPONS TO BE CARRIED WITHIN THESE WALLS.
WE'RE NOT TAKING YOUR WEAPONS, THEY'RE STILL YOURS, WE JUST ASK THAT IF YOU LIVE WITHIN THESE WALLS, YOU ALLOW US TO STORE THEM HERE.
IF YOU GUYS WILL PLEASE REMOVE ALL WEAPONS AND PLACE THEM ON THE PORCH, OLIVIA HERE WILL BRING THEM ALL INSIDE.

I'D LIKE TO KEEP MY SWORD WITH ME. IT HAS SENTIMENTAL VALUE.

AGAIN, WE'RE NOT TAKING YOUR WEAPONS, JUST STORING THEM HERE. AND I'M SORRY, BUT A WEAPON IS A WEAPON...
...AND I'M TOLD YOU'RE QUITE DEADLY WITH THAT SWORD.

OH, DOUGLAS. A WEAPON IS A WEAPON? ANYTHING CAN BE A WEAPON. TO MOST PEOPLE A HAMMER'D BE MORE DEADLY THAN THAT SWORD, YOU LET PEOPLE KEEP THOSE.
I'VE GOT KNIVES IN MY KITCHEN AREN'T MUCH SMALLER THAN THAT. LET THE WOMAN KEEP HER SWORD.

YOU DO NOT CARRY IT WITH YOU. KEEP IT IN YOUR HOUSE.
IN FACT, I WANT TO SEE IT HANGING OVER YOUR MANTEL. IT'S RETIRED AS LONG AS YOU'RE WITHIN THESE WALLS.

SCOTT? YOU AWAKE?
THEY TOLD ME YOU WERE AWAKE.
I AM.

YOU FEELING OKAY? HELL OF A DAY TODAY, HUH?

YEAH, ONE FOR THE BOOKS. DOC'S GOT ME ON SOME PAIN KILLERS. NOT WORKING THAT GREAT, BUT THEY DO ENOUGH.
I WAS PRETTY OUT OF IT. I REMEMBER AARON CAME AND SAVED US--BUT HE HAD NEW PEOPLE WITH HIM, RIGHT?
SEEMED LIKE A LOT, BUT THAT CAN'T BE RIGHT.

NO, IT IS. AARON FOUND A GROUP OF TWELVE. WOMEN, KIDS... ALL NORMAL. AT LEAST THEY SEEM THAT WAY.
APPARENTLY THEY'VE HOLED UP IN A FEW PLACES FOR A LONG TIME--BUT THEY'VE MOSTLY SURVIVED ON THEIR OWN.
IT'S CRAZY.

TWELVE? THAT'S A SMALL ARMY.
THAT SURE MAKES ME A LITTLE UNEASY. I DON'T--
HEY, SCOTT--JUST CHECKING IN TO MAKE SURE YOU'RE DOING OKAY.

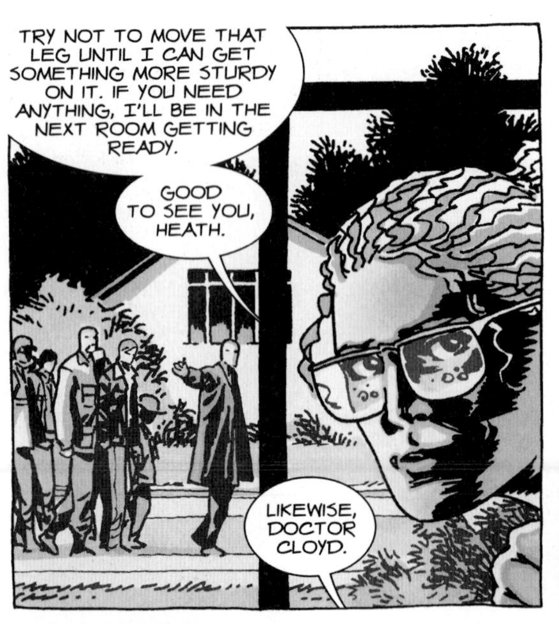
TRY NOT TO MOVE THAT LEG UNTIL I CAN GET SOMETHING MORE STURDY ON IT. IF YOU NEED ANYTHING, I'LL BE IN THE NEXT ROOM GETTING READY.
GOOD TO SEE YOU, HEATH.
LIKEWISE, DOCTOR CLOYD.

THIS HOUSE IS THE INFIRMARY. WE ACTUALLY HAVE THREE DOCTORS HERE IN THE COMMUNITY, ONE A SURGEON.

THANKS TO HEATH AND THE OTHER RUNNERS, WE HAVE SOME STATE OF THE ART EQUIPMENT. IT'S QUITE NICE.

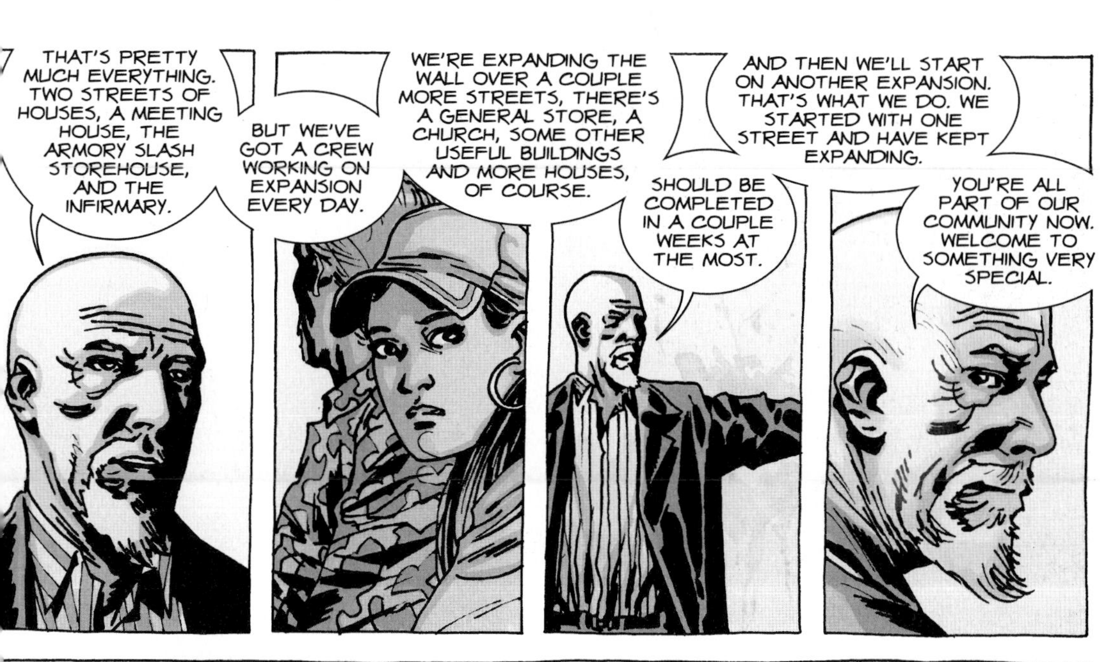
THAT'S PRETTY MUCH EVERYTHING. TWO STREETS OF HOUSES, A MEETING HOUSE, THE ARMORY SLASH STOREHOUSE, AND THE INFIRMARY.
BUT WE'VE GOT A CREW WORKING ON EXPANSION EVERY DAY.
WE'RE EXPANDING THE WALL OVER A COUPLE MORE STREETS, THERE'S A GENERAL STORE, A CHURCH, SOME OTHER USEFUL BUILDINGS AND MORE HOUSES, OF COURSE.
SHOULD BE COMPLETED IN A COUPLE WEEKS AT THE MOST.
AND THEN WE'LL START ON ANOTHER EXPANSION. THAT'S WHAT WE DO. WE STARTED WITH ONE STREET AND HAVE KEPT EXPANDING.
YOU'RE ALL PART OF OUR COMMUNITY NOW. WELCOME TO SOMETHING VERY SPECIAL.

THESE ARE THE LAST OF THE VACANTS. OBVIOUSLY NOT ENOUGH FOR ALL OF YOU, AT LEAST NOT UNTIL THE EXPANSION.
I'LL LET YOU DISCUSS HOW YOU'D LIKE TO DIVIDE THEM AMONGST YOURSELVES.

WE'VE GOT THREE HOUSES TO SPLIT AMONG US? HOLY *CRAP*-- RIGHT?
I DON'T REALLY CARE HOW WE SPLIT UP AS LONG AS THE COUPLES STAY TOGETHER, OBVIOUSLY.
YEAH, REALLY-- I'LL SLEEP WHEREVER. I DON'T CARE.

FINE, I'LL TAKE HOUSE ONE WITH CARL, ANDREA AND MORGAN. HOUSE TWO CAN BE MAGGIE, GLENN, SOPHIA AND MICHONNE.
THAT LEAVES ABRAHAM, ROSITA, GABRIEL... AND EUGENE IN HOUSE THREE. EVERYONE OKAY WITH THAT?

FINE WITH ME. LET'S UNLOAD THE TRUCK AND START GETTING THINGS SET UP.

THIS IS SOMETHING ELSE, HUH?
Y'KNOW... IT REALLY IS. I'M IMPRESSED.

LISTEN, I DIDN'T MEAN TO PUT EUGENE IN YOUR HOUSE. I WASN'T THINKING THERE. I KNOW THINGS ARE STILL TENSE.
THANKS FOR NOT CAUSING A FUSS.

I NEED TO TALK TO HIM, HE WAS A CLOSE FRIEND BEFORE I FOUND OUT HOW FULL OF IT HE WAS. OR AT LEAST, WHAT PASSES FOR A CLOSE FRIEND THESE DAYS.
AND HE BROUGHT US HERE. SO THAT'S GOTTA COUNT FOR SOMETHING. THING IS, I DIDN'T CAUSE A FUSS BECAUSE WE'RE NOT SLEEPING IN OUR HOUSE TONIGHT.

WHAT?
WHAT ARE YOU THINKING?

I'M THINKING THEY TOOK OUR WEAPONS AND NOW THEY'RE SPLITTING US UP. COULD BE NOTHING, COULD BE SOMETHING.
I SAY WE SNEAK THROUGH THE BACKYARDS AFTER DARK, WE ALL SLEEP IN YOUR HOUSE WITHOUT THEM KNOWING.
JUST TO BE ON THE SAFE SIDE.

YEAH... I CAN GET BEHIND THAT. AS A PRECAUTION, FOR THE FIRST FEW DAYS.
LET'S SPREAD THE WORD.

CARL? WHY AREN'T YOU ASLEEP?
CAN'T. IT'S WEIRD HERE. NOT NORMAL. I CAN'T SLEEP BECAUSE OF IT.

ALL THAT RUNNING AND PLAYING YOU DID? I FIGURED YOU'D BE EXHAUSTED. PUT RIGHT TO SLEEP.
YOU OKAY? ANYTHING YOU WANT TO TALK ABOUT?

I DON'T THINK THE OTHER KIDS ARE GOING TO LIKE ME.
I'M NOT LIKE THEM, DAD.

NONSENSE. YOU'VE JUST FORGOTTEN THAT YOU'RE A KID-- THAT'S ALL. IT'LL ALL COME BACK TO YOU.
DON'T WORRY. THIS PLACE IS GOING TO BE GOOD FOR US. YOU'LL SEE.

I DON'T KNOW. MAYBE.
I SURE HOPE S--
KNOCK! KNOCK!

IS THAT THE FRONT DOOR?
STAY HERE.

I'VE GOT IT. STAY PUT.

I GOT IT. I'M SURE IT'S NOTHING.

HI, RICK. SORRY TO BOTHER YOU.

MEANT TO TELL YOU EARLIER BUT WE'RE DOING A HALLOWEEN THING TOMORROW. WE'VE GOT CANDY FOR ALL THE HOUSES BACK AT THE SUPPLY HOUSE. ALL THE KIDS ARE DRESSING UP.
WANTED TO MAKE SURE I TOLD YOU TONIGHT SO YOU COULD BE THINKING ABOUT THE KIDS' COSTUMES-- ALTHOUGH--
HEH.
I GUESS CARL IS ALREADY DRESSED AS A COWBOY. SO THAT WORKS.

YEAH. THAT'LL BE FUN FOR THE KIDS. THANKS FOR LETTING ME KNOW.

HM. ALL IN ONE HOUSE?
SMART.
MUCH SAFER IF WE *DO* TURN OUT TO BE DANGEROUS.

HAVE A GOOD NIGHT, RICK.

HAVING A GOOD TIME?
LOOK AT THAT LITTLE COWBOY-- VERY COOL.

UGH.
DON'T MIND HIM. HE'S JUST HERE FOR THE CANDY.

WHO ISN'T?
I HOPE YOUR PEOPLE ARE ENJOYING THIS--A HOLIDAY. I'M SURE THAT'S NOT SOMETHING YOU GUYS HAVE CELEBRATED MANY OF.

REALLY, CARL. I'M SURE WE CAN THROW SOMETHING TOGETHER. IT WOULD ONLY TAKE A MINUTE.
NO. THIS IS STUPID. I DON'T WANT TO DRESS UP.

I'LL BE HONEST WITH YOU, DOUGLAS. WE'RE STILL A LITTLE SKEPTICAL, AS YOU LEARNED LAST NIGHT--BUT THIS WHOLE PLACE IS REALLY GROWING ON US. YOU'VE DONE SOMETHING REMARKABLE HERE.
I NEED TO COMPARE CALENDARS WITH YOU. ANDREA WAS KEEPING ONE FOR US FOR A WHILE- BUT IT'S SPOTTY AT BEST.
ARE YOU SURE IT'S OCTOBER THIRTY-FIRST?

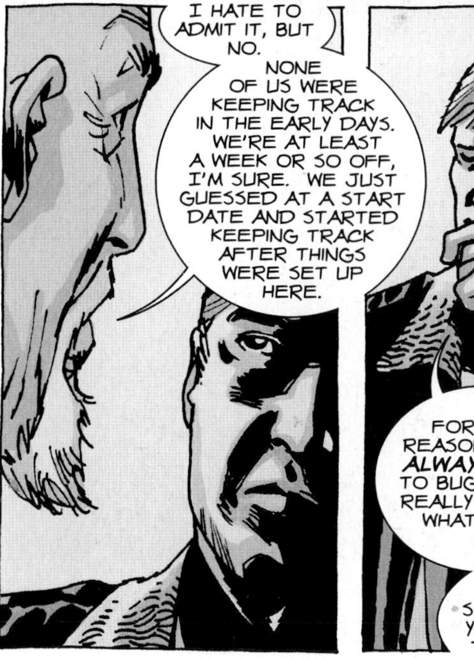
I HATE TO ADMIT IT, BUT NO.
NONE OF US WERE KEEPING TRACK IN THE EARLY DAYS. WE'RE AT LEAST A WEEK OR SO OFF, I'M SURE. WE JUST GUESSED AT A START DATE AND STARTED KEEPING TRACK AFTER THINGS WERE SET UP HERE.

FOR SOME REASON, THAT'S ALWAYS GOING TO BUG ME. NOT REALLY KNOWING WHAT DAY IT IS.
WE NEED TO ASK AROUND, I'M SURE THERE'S SOME WAY YOU CAN USE THE MOON TO FIGURE IT ALL OUT.

WHAT'S THE MATTER?
SHE THOUGHT I WAS A COWBOY, TOO.
THIS IS *STUPID.* I'M GOING HOME.

PLEASE EXCUSE ME.
NO WORRIES. WE'LL HAVE PLENTY OF TIME TO TALK LATER.

CARL, SLOW DOWN!
WAIT!

WHY ARE YOU GOING HOME?

THE COSTUMES, THE CANDY--EVERYONE WALKING AROUND, ACTING LIKE ***NOTHING'S*** HAPPENING AROUND THEM.
THEY'RE ALL STUPID. THE ROAMERS DIDN'T GO AWAY BECAUSE YOU CAN'T ***SEE*** THEM.
I HATE THIS PLACE, DAD. IT DOESN'T FEEL ***REAL.***
IT FEELS LIKE EVERYONE IS PLAYING ***PRETEND.***

CARL, LISTEN TO ME... PLEASE.
YOU CAN LET YOURSELF ENJOY THIS. I KNOW YOU WANT TO.

GO, HAVE FUN, BE A KID. WE'RE SAFE HERE. YOU CAN LET YOUR GUARD DOWN, RELAX--WE DON'T HAVE TO LIVE LIKE WE USED TO.
THINGS ARE DIFFERENT NOW.
BUT DAD... WHAT ABOUT WHEN WE LEAVE HERE?
I DON'T WANT TO GET USED TO THIS-- IT'LL MAKE US WEAK. I DON'T WANT TO DIE.

C'MON... I'LL TAKE YOU HOME.

HE OKAY?
FINE. HE'S INSIDE READING. CAN'T EVER REALLY GET ONTO HIM FOR DOING THAT, Y'KNOW?
TELL ME SOMETHING-- WHY ARE YOU DOING THIS AT MIDDAY?
HALLOWEEN AT NIGHT IS SCARY, RICK. I FIGURED IT BEST TO AVOID ANY OF THAT.
MIND IF I BEND YOUR EAR A LITTLE? I THINK I COULD USE YOUR ADVICE.
REALLY? REGARDING WHAT?
PLACEMENT. YOU WERE EASY. ABRAHAM IS ON HIS WAY TO SECURITY AND CONSTRUCTION. MORGAN IS GOING TO BE A CHEF, GLENN IS GOING TO BE A RUNNER, REPLACING SCOTT FOR THE TIME BEING.
MAGGIE IS GOING TO BE A TEACHER, IT'LL BE GOOD TO HAVE TWO OF THOSE. ROSITA IS GOING TO WORK WITH THE DOCTORS AND TRAIN WITH THEM. EUGENE IS GOING TO BE A COMMUNITY PLANNER. GABRIEL... WE'LL HAVE A CHURCH IN A MATTER OF DAYS.
I'M TORN ON MICHONNE. SHE WAS A LAWYER--AND I UNDERSTAND SHE'S TOUGH AS NAILS.

...PUTTING IT MILDLY.

RIGHT. SO WHILE I DON'T THINK WE NEED A LAWYER PER SE--I THINK YOU COULD PROBABLY USE HELP AS CONSTABLE, AND SHE'D BE MUSCLE--AND BRAINS AS FAR AS UPHOLDING THE LAW GOES.
THAT SOUND GOOD TO YOU?

THAT SOUND PERFEC

THE OTHER ONE I'M HAVING TROUBLE WITH IS ANDREA.
SHE'S A SHARPSHOOTER-- THAT TELLS ME SECURITY, BUT WHEN I THINK ABOUT IT--THAT SEEMS LIKE A WASTE OF HER TALENTS.
SO I'M AT A LOSS.
WHO'S OUR LOOKOUT?

OUR WHAT?

YOU DON'T HAVE A LOOKOUT?

YOU RECRUIT PEOPLE, DOUGLAS. AARON AND ERIC--THEY WATCH THEM, MAKE SURE THEY'RE OKAY. THEN YOU BRING THEM IN, MAKE SURE THEY'RE OKAY, SAFE--NOT CRAZY.
WHAT IF SOMEONE FOUND YOU? WHAT THEN?
OR EVEN WORSE--WHAT IF IT WAS A BIG GROUP-- BIG ENOUGH TO ACTUALLY MOUNT AN ATTACK ON THIS PLACE? WHAT IF SOMEONE WANTED TO TAKE IT OVER?
YOU HAVE TO KNOW HOW DESIRABLE A PLACE LIKE THIS WOULD LOOK ON THE OUTSIDE. WHEN WE WERE IN THE PRISON--THAT WAS A BIG CONCERN. SOMEONE WE DIDN'T WANT IN--WANTING IN.
AND IT EVENTUALLY HAPPENED.

IT'S NOT LIKE THAT'S SOMETHING WE'VE NEVER CONSIDERED--BUT I ALWAYS THOUGHT THE WALL WAS ENOUGH.
I THINK YOU'RE RIGHT THOUGH. WE NEED A LOOKOUT.

THERE'S A BELL TOWER UP THE STREET A WAYS FROM HERE--SAW IT ON THE WAY IN. SOME KIND OF GOVERNMENT BUILDING.
THAT WOULD MAKE A GOOD POSITION.

OKAY THEN.
ANDREA IS OUR LOOKOUT.

SOMEONE'S IN HERE!
SORRY!

IT'S NICE, AND THEY SEEMED LIKE GOOD PEOPLE.
EXCUS ME.

NO, NOT ONE MORE. NO MORE. YOU'VE HAD ENOUGH. YOU'RE SUPPOSED TO BE ASLEEP RIGHT NOW!
AW, MOM! BUT I HAVE SO MUCH CANDY!

DON'T BOTHER. ABRAHAM AND ROSITA ARE IN THERE. I THINK THEY'RE TAKING A SHOWER.
AND I'M NEXT.

YOU GONNA BRUSH YOUR TEETH? I CAN MOVE SOME OF THE DISHES OUT OF THE WAY.
SORRY, I ALWAYS HATE LEAVING THEM OVERNIGHT. ALSO-- I'M DOING DISHES! ISN'T THAT NEAT? I ACTUALLY MISSED THIS.

IT'S OKAY, GLENN.
I GIVE UP. DON'T WORR ABOUT IT.

I CAN'T BELIEVE CARL'S SLEEPING THROUGH ALL THIS. THAT HOUSE IS A CIRCUS.
ME NEITHER. I'M THINKING TOMORROW WE SPREAD OUT TO THE OTHER HOUSES.

HEY-- LOOK AT THAT.

WEIRD, RIGHT?
I KNOW, EVERYTHING JUST SEEMS... FAKE.

Y'KNOW... CARL WAS SAYING THAT EARLIER TODAY.
I GUESS AFTER EVERYTHING WE'VE BEEN THROUGH, THIS JUST DOESN'T SEEM POSSIBLE.
I MEAN... I'M HERE AND I CAN HARDLY BELIEVE IT.
THIS WON'T LAST... IT *NEVER* DOES.
ENJOY IT WHILE YOU CAN--AND PRAY IT DOESN'T MAKE US TOO SOFT TO SURVIVE WHEN IT'S OVER.

AM I THE ONLY PERSON THINKING ABOUT THIS LIKE IT COULD ACTUALLY BE SOMETHING THAT *LASTS?*
I WAS THE SKEPTIC--WHAT HAPPENED?
WHY COULDN'T WE SPEND THE REST OF OUR LIVES HERE? IS THAT IMPOSSIBLE?

THERE'S JUST SO MUCH THAT COULD GO WRONG.
AN ORGANIZED GROUP COULD ATTACK, A HERD COULD TEAR THROUGH HERE. FIRE. STORMS... ANY NUMBER OF THINGS.
AND LOOK AT US. YOU REALLY THINK THEY'RE GOING TO LET US STAY HERE ONCE THEY REALIZE HOW FUCKED UP WE ALL ARE?
ARE YOU KIDDING?
HAVE YOU BEEN WATCHING THESE PEOPLE? ANYONE HALF DANGEROUS THEY SEND OUT TO WORK CONSTRUCTION OUTSIDE THE WALL EVERY DAY.
IF THEY EVER TRY TO MAKE US LEAVE WE'LL JUST TAKE THIS PLACE FROM THEM AND MAKE IT OURS.

I MEAN IT.
I'M NOT GOING TO LET THESE PEOPLE--

UH...
RICK?

WHAT?
OH.

SORRY TO STARTLE YOU. I SWEAR I *DON'T* MAKE A HABIT OF SLINKING AROUND AFTER DARK.
RICK, YOU MIND IF I BORROW ANDREA FOR A BIT?
NO. NOT AT ALL...

WHAT CAN I DO FOR YOU, DOUGLAS?
NOW THAT'S NOT WHAT THIS IS ABOUT AT ALL. I'M HERE TO ASK WHAT I CAN DO FOR **YOU.**
IS THERE ANYTHING YOU NEED--ANYTHING YOU **WANT?** ANYTHING YOU'RE UNHAPPY ABOUT? I CAN FIX PRETTY MUCH... **WHATEVER** AILS YOU.

ARE YOU GOING TO TRY AND TELL ME THIS IS SOMETHING YOU'RE ASKING **EVERYONE** AGAIN?

WHAT WOULD YOU SAY IF I SAID IT **WASN'T**--THAT THIS WAS JUST FOR **YOU?**
I'D SAY THAT YOU'RE A MARRIED MAN AND I'M **EXTREMELY** UNINTERESTED...
...WITH ALL DUE RESPECT.

AND TO THAT I'D SAY THAT IF ME BEING MARRIED IS WHAT'S HOLDING YOU BACK--DON'T LET IT.
I'M IN A PURELY POLITICAL MARRIAGE. MY WIFE DOESN'T CARE WHAT I DO AND I FEEL THE SAME WAY ABOUT HER. IF WE DIDN'T THINK THE KIDS NEEDED THE STABILITY I'D HAVE LEFT HER LONG AGO.
THERE'S **NOTHING** THERE.

...

I'M VERY LONELY.

I'M JUST NOT INTERESTED. I'M SORRY.

NO, GLENN. IT'S NOT FAIR--NOT TO US. YOU CAN'T DO THIS. DAMN IT, YOU CAN'T!
THIS IS WHAT I'M GOOD AT, MAGGIE. WHEN WE WERE NEAR ATLANTA I WAS ALWAYS GOING IN FOR SUPPLIES. IT'S WHAT I'M BEST SUITED FOR.
THEY NEED ME!

I DON'T GIVE A DAMN WHAT THEY NEED!

GIVE IT A MINUTE. BIG FIGHT GOING ON IN THERE.
OH? WHAT HAPPENED?
GLENN TOLD MAGGIE HE'S GOING TO BE A SUPPLY RUNNER GOING INTO WASHINGTON.
IT'S NOT PRETTY.

GOT IT.

I'LL WAIT. IT'S NOT TOO COLD TONIGHT.
WHAT'S GOT YOU SO HAPPY?

THAT CREEPY OLD BASTARD JUST HIT ON ME.

WHAT?
REALLY? ISN'T HE MARRIED?

SOME KIND OF POLITICAL NONSENSE, HE CLAIMS. A LOVELESS MARRIAGE.
SOUNDED LIKE BULLSHIT TO ME.

WOW, THIS IS JUST... WE'VE NEVER HAD THIS BEFORE.
I KNOW, THIS IS THE FIRST TIME SOMEONE'S HIT ON ME SINCE ALL THIS STARTED...

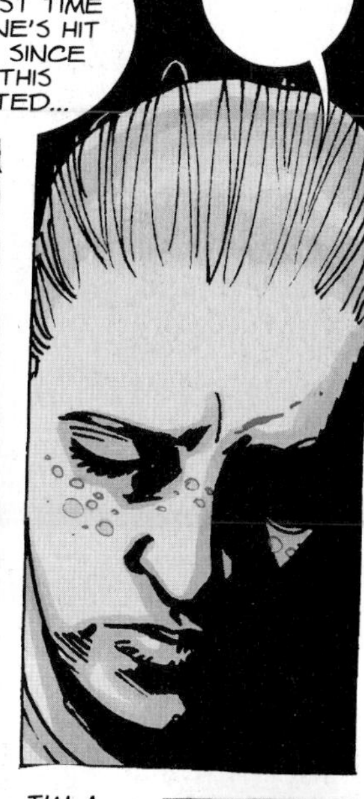
...

I'M A HORRIBLE PERSON. DALE'S BODY IS BARELY COLD AND I'M HERE LAUGHING ABOUT GETTING HIT ON.
WHAT IS WRONG WITH ME?
NOTHING.

THERE'S NOT ENOUGH TIME TO DWELL ON THE PAST. I KNOW YOU MISS DALE. YOU KNOW YOU MISS DALE.
DOESN'T MEAN YOU CAN'T BE A LITTLE HAPPY EVERY NOW AND THEN.

THANKS, RICK.

OH, UH... DIDN'T KNOW YOU GUYS WERE OUT HERE.

I'M NOT WAITING FOR ROUND TWO. I'M GETTING WHILE THE GETTING'S GOOD. GOOD NIGHT, ALL.
AND... I MUST SAY, I DON'T SEE THE NEED FOR US TO ALL SLEEP IN *THIS* HOUSE TOMORROW NIGHT. IT'S CRAMPED AND THEY KNOW WE'RE DOING IT.
AGREED... AND SLEEP WELL.
SORRY FOR THE DISRUPTION.

DON'T WORRY ABOUT IT. KIND OF NICE, ACTUALLY... IF I'M COMPLETELY HONEST.
DON'T BE A SMART-ASS.

NO, I'M SERIOUS. WE DIDN'T HAVE *TIME* FOR DOMESTIC DISPUTES BEFORE.
IT'S GOOD TO SEE THINGS ARE CHANGING.

EASY FOR YOU TO SAY.

BANG!
BANG!
BANG!
BANG!
BANG! BANG! BANG!

I'M THROUGH WITH YOU.

MORNING, KIDS.

HI, CONSTABLE.

SMILE, KID. IF YOU'RE NOT CAREFUL, YOUR FACE WILL GET STUCK THAT WAY.

ABRAHAM, ROSITA--HEY. OUT FOR A WALK?
YES, SIR. ISN'T THIS PLACE JUST SOMETHING ELSE?

WE'VE BEEN OUT, LOOKING AROUND, TRYING TO RELAX, MAKE THE MOST OF THE DAY. TOMORROW I START ON THE CONSTRUCTION CREW--COMPLETING THE NEW EXPANSION SO ROSITA AND I CAN HAVE A PLACE OF OUR OWN.
OH, I CAN'T WAIT! THIS PLACE IS SO EXCITING. IT'S GOING TO BE NICE HAVING A PLACE ALL TO OURSELVES.
I HEAR YOU.

OF COURSE, I'VE GOT TO WORK AS A NURSE--OR DOCTOR'S ASSISTANT, WHATEVER, IN RETURN. NOT BIG ON THAT.
I GET SQUEAMISH. YES, EVEN AFTER EVERYTHING WE'VE SEEN.
I WASN'T GOING TO SAY ANYTHING. YOU DON'T HAVE TO EXPLAIN ANYTHING TO ME.
YOU BE SQUEAMISH ALL YOU WANT.

YOU GOING TO THIS DINNER PARTY THING THAT DOUGLAS IS THROWING TONIGHT?

SURE. OF COURSE I AM.
ISN'T EVERYONE INVITED? THAT'S WHAT I HEARD-- SOME KIND OF MEET AND GREET THING.
GLAD IT'S NOT BEING HELD AT MY PLACE.

ARE YOU HAVING FUN?
NO, OF COURSE YOU AREN'T. AT LEAST GET SOMETHING TO EAT, CARL. WHEN'S THE LAST TIME YOU HAD A HAMBURGER?
THEY LOOK GROSS, HOW LONG WERE THEY FROZEN? THEY TASTE FUNNY.
IT'S ALL IN YOUR HEAD, SON. THEY TASTE FINE.

I DIDN'T THINK I'D SEE YOU HERE, DOCTOR CLOYD.
I'M JUST MAKING AN APPEARANCE. I'VE GOT TO GO CHECK IN ON SCOTT LATER. HE'S STILL RUNNING A FEVER, WHICH HAS ME WORRIED.

RICK, HI. I JUST WANTED TO SAY, ABOUT THE OTHER DAY-- NO HARD FEELINGS, OKAY? KIDS, Y'KNOW?
OH, THANKS... NICHOLAS, WAS IT? YEAH, NO WORRIES, MAN. I APPRECIATE YOU COMING UP TO ME LIKE THIS.

NICKY BOY!

WHERE YOU BEEN HIDING, MAN? I HAVEN'T SEEN YOU IN DAYS!
HOW'S MIKEY AND PAULA?
FINE. THEY'RE AROUND HERE SOMEWHERE.

CAN I GO FIND MIKEY?
ASK YOUR FATHER, RON.

GO AHEAD, KID. RUN ALONG.

WE WERE CLEARING OUT THE GYMNASIUM--AND WE GOT OVERWHELMED. LEFT THE GUY IN THERE. WE THOUGHT HE WAS DEAD.
LATER, WE WENT IN THERE--AND HE WAS ALL "WHAT TOOK YOU SO LONG?" HE'D KILLED EVERY DAMN LAST ONE OF THEM!
NO SHIT? THAT'S AMAZING.

HAVING A GOOD TIME?
YEAH, IT'S UNUSUAL--LIKE WE'RE IN ANOTHER DIMENSION OR SOMETHING... BUT YEAH. WE'RE HAVING A GREAT TIME.
YOU SEEN ANDREA AROUND?
SHE'S OUT BACK.

WOW, WORD DOES TRAVEL FAST AROUND HERE. NO. I WAS A CLERK IN A LAWYER'S OFFICE BEFORE. I'D NEVER EVEN FIRED A GUN BEFORE.
I MEAN, YOU JUST POINT AND SHOOT RIGHT? IT'S NOT THAT HARD.
OH, YEAH-- IT'S JUST THAT SIMPLE.
WELL, YEAH-- THERE'S OBVIOUSLY MORE TO IT. BUT I JUST TOOK TO IT REALLY WELL, I SUPPOSE. IT DIDN'T EVEN REALLY TAKE THAT MUCH TRAINING.

THE THING ABOUT LIVING HERE THAT WILL PROBABLY SURPRISE YOU-- OR MAYBE NOT, IS THAT PEOPLE GET BORED HERE, REALLY EASILY.
YOU SHOULD DO A DEMONSTRATION OR SOMETHING.

A DEMONSTRATION? HA. I'M SORRY, BUT NO. THAT WOULD BE BORING.
IT'S NOT LIKE I CAN SHOOT CIGARETTES OUT OF PEOPLE'S MOUTHS OR ANYTHING. I'VE JUST GOT PRETTY GOOD AIM. IT'S NOT VERY SHOWY.
I CAN SPLATTER A ROAMER'S HEAD FROM A GOOD DISTANCE. I DOUBT THE PEOPLE HERE WANT TO SEE THAT.

ANDREA, SPENCER. I'M JUST GOING AROUND TAKING REQUESTS. CAN I GET YOU ANYTHING TO DRINK?
DO YOU NEED ANYTHING, ANDREA?

I'M FINE, THANKS.

WELL, THEN--CARRY ON YOU TWO. SORRY FOR THE INTERRUPTION.
SON, HAVE YOU SEEN YOUR MOTHER?
SHE'S OVER BY THE GRILL, TALKING TO DAVID.

I KNOW, ISN'T HE JUST SO HANDSOME? SPENCER IS SUCH AN ATTRACTIVE YOUNG MAN.
MAYBE TOO ATTRACTIVE, IF YOU KNOW WHAT I'M SAYING. I COULD SEE HIM GOING OUT ON SCOUTING MISSIONS WITH ERIC AND AARON...
...IF YOU KNOW WHAT I'M SAYING.

YOU SPEAK TOO SOON, BARBARA. JUST MINUTES AGO I SAW HIM TALKING TO THE GIRL IN YOUR CAMP, MICHONNE. THE SHARP SHOOTER.
ANDREA.

HER? FUNNY.
DOUGLAS CLEARLY HAS HIS EYE ON HER. THAT'S GOING TO BE INTERESTING.

NEVER A DULL MOMENT AROUND HERE. I TELL YOU.
YOU'RE SINGLE, MICHONNE? WE REALLY NEED TO FIX YOU UP.

YOU KNOW HEATH IS SINGLE?

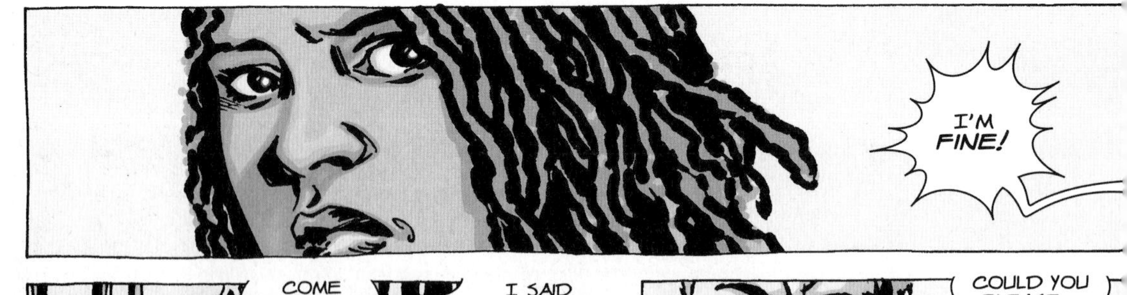
I'M FINE!

COME ON, WE'RE LEAVING.
I SAID I'M FINE! I'M NOT GOING ANYWHERE!

COULD YOU PLEASE--
I'VE GOT IT UNDER CONTROL.

I'LL TAKE CARE OF THIS.
GLENN, C'MON. WE'RE GOING OUTSIDE.

ALL OUR KIDS ARE HERE, GLENN. JESUS.
I'M SORRY.
I'M SORRY.

JUST... GET HIM HOME. I'LL MAKE SURE SOPHIA MAKES IT BACK OKAY.
OKAY, THANKS, RICK.

A LITTLE TOO MUCH CELEBRATION--AND WHO CAN BLAME HIM?
LET'S NOT LET THE NIGHT GO TO WASTE, EVERYONE. CARRY ON.

LOOK AT YOU! GO MINGLE, JEEZ. WE'RE SUPPOSED TO BE GETTING TO KNOW THESE PEOPLE.

ALL YOU'VE DONE AND YOU CAN'T HANDLE A LITTLE DINNER PARTY?

THAT'S NOT IT. IT'S *TOMORROW.*
A FEW DAYS INSIDE... AND I ALREADY DON'T WANT TO GO ON THE OTHER SIDE OF THAT WALL.

MICHONNE-- WAIT! ARE YOU LEAVING?

OH, SORRY. I KNOW IT'S STILL EARLY, BUT I WAS GOING TO CALL IT A NIGHT.

OH, I TOTALLY UNDERSTAND THAT. ONE THING THOUGH, WE ALWAYS LIKE TO COOK THINGS FOR THE NEW ARRIVALS.
I REALLY WANTED TO MAKE SOMETHING SPECIAL FOR YOU. IS THERE ANYTHING IN PARTICULAR YOU'D LIKE? SOMETHING YOU MAYBE HAVEN'T HAD IN A WHILE?
REALLY, YOU DON'T HAVE TO. I APPRECIATE IT, BUT I'D RATHER YOU DIDN'T GO TO THE TROUBLE.

IT'S NO TROUBLE AT ALL, REALLY. PLEASE TELL ME WHAT YOU'D LIKE.
I'VE BEEN SO WORRIED THAT I'D COOK SOMETHING YOU WOULDN'T ENJOY.

WORRIED?!
THIS IS WHAT YOU WORRY ABOUT?!

REALLY, THANKS FOR HAVING US. THIS HAS BEEN *GREAT.*
THANKS FOR COMING. I'M SORRY YOU HAVE TO LEAVE SO SOON.

IT'S STARTING TO GET LATE, AND I'VE GOT TO GET THIS GIRL BACK TO HER HOUSE FIRST.
...AND CHECK IN ON GLENN.

I HOPE HE'S OKAY.
IF HE'S STILL AWAKE, DO MAKE SURE YOU TELL HIM THAT NO ONE IS UPSET WITH HIM. I DON'T WANT HIM TO FEEL EMBARRASSED. WE'VE *ALL* BEEN THERE.

YOU WOULDN'T BELIEVE...
OH? SOUNDS LIKE YOU'VE GOT SOME INTERESTING STORIES FOR ME SOME TIME.
I'LL KEEP THAT IN MIND.
GOOD LUCK PRYING THOSE OUT OF ME.
GOOD NIGHT, RICK.
CARL. SOPHIA.

MORGAN? I DIDN'T KNOW YOU'D LEFT THE PARTY, TOO.
YEAH, A WHILE AGO.

WASN'T EASY.
SEEING PEOPLE... *HAPPY.*

YEAH, HAPPY... AND TALKING ABOUT COMPLETE AND UTTER BULLSHIT.
I KIND OF MADE A SCENE WHEN I WAS LEAVING.

OH?
CAN'T PICTURE IT? I USED TO BE KNOWN FOR THAT KIND OF THING.
I GUESS BEING HERE HAS BROUGHT IT BACK.

MADE ME FEEL SO...
...ALONE.

IS MY DAD OKAY?
HE'S FINE, DON'T WORRY. HE JUST GOT A LITTLE SICK, THAT'S ALL.

HEY, COME IN.
ANYONE HAVE ANYTHING TO SAY ABOUT OUR "SCENE?"

NO, NOTHING AT ALL REALLY. DRUNK GUYS MUST BE COMMON.
WHERE IS HE?

IN THE BACK.
DID YOU KIDS HAVE FUN?
YEAH.
NO.

SHUT THE DOOR SO THE KIDS DON'T HEAR.
FEELING BETTER?

I'VE HAD A MIRACULOUS RECOVERY.

WELL?
WHAT DID YOU FIND?

THEY'RE LOCKED UP, BUT IT'S JUST A ROOM, NOT A SAFE OR ANYTHING. I COULD BREAK IN THROUGH A WINDOW--BUT THEY'D KNOW SOMEONE HAD GOTTEN IN.
WE'LL FIGURE SOMETHING OUT. I'M SURE I CA DO IT.

I *KNOW*. THAT'S WHY I SENT YOU.
I DON'T CARE WHAT THESE PEOPLE SAY. THIS PLACE IS TOO IMPORTANT... I'M *NOT* TAKING ANY CHANCES.
I WANT OUR GUNS BACK--AND YOU'RE GOING TO GET THEM FOR US.

TO BE CONTINUED...

HE ASTOUNDING WOLF-MAN

OL. 1 TP
SBN: 978-1-58240-862-0
$14.99
OL. 2 TP
SBN: 978-1-60706-007-9
$14.99
OL. 3 TP
SBN: 978-1-60706-111-3
$16.99

ATTLE POPE

OL. 1: GENESIS TP
SBN: 978-1-58240-572-8
$14.99
OL. 2: MAYHEM TP
SBN: 978-1-58240-529-2
$12.99
OL. 3: PILLOW TALK TP
SBN: 978-1-58240-677-0
$12.99
OL. 4: WRATH OF GOD TP
SBN: 978-1-58240-751-7
$9.99

RIT

OL. 1: OLD SOLDIER TP
SBN: 978-1-58240-678-7
$14.99
OL. 2: AWOL
SBN: 978-1-58240-864-4
$14.99
OL. 3: FUBAR
SBN: 978-1-60706-061-1
$16.99

APES

OL. 1: PUNCHING THE CLOCK TP
SBN: 978-1-58240-756-2
$17.99

HAUNT

OL. 1 TP
SBN: 978-1-60706-154-0
$9.99

NVINCIBLE

OL. 1: FAMILY MATTERS TP
SBN: 978-1-58240-711-1
$12.99
VOL. 2: EIGHT IS ENOUGH TP
ISBN: 978-1-58240-347-2
$12.99
VOL. 3: PERFECT STRANGERS TP
ISBN: 978-1-58240-793-7
$12.99
VOL. 4: HEAD OF THE CLASS TP
ISBN: 978-1-58240-440-2
$14.95
VOL. 5: THE FACTS OF LIFE TP
ISBN: 978-1-58240-554-4
$14.99
VOL. 6: A DIFFERENT WORLD TP
ISBN: 978-1-58240-579-7
$14.99
VOL. 7: THREE'S COMPANY TP
ISBN: 978-1-58240-656-5
$14.99
VOL. 8: MY FAVORITE MARTIAN TP
ISBN: 978-1-58240-683-1
$14.99
VOL. 9: OUT OF THIS WORLD TP
ISBN: 978-1-58240-827-9
$14.99
VOL. 10: WHO'S THE BOSS TP
ISBN: 978-1-60706-013-0
$16.99
VOL. 11: HAPPY DAYS TP
ISBN: 978-1-60706-062-8
$16.99
VOL. 12: STILL STANDING TP
ISBN: 978-1-60706-166-3
$16.99
VOL. 13: GROWING PAINS TP
ISBN: 978-1-60706-251-6
$16.99
ULTIMATE COLLECTION, VOL. 1 HC
ISBN 978-1-58240-500-1
$34.95
ULTIMATE COLLECTION, VOL. 2 HC
ISBN: 978-1-58240-594-0
$34.99
ULTIMATE COLLECTION, VOL. 3 HC
ISBN: 978-1-58240-763-0
$34.99
ULTIMATE COLLECTION, VOL. 4 HC
ISBN: 978-1-58240-989-4
$34.99
ULTIMATE COLLECTION, VOL. 5 HC
ISBN: 978-1-60706-116-8
$34.99
THE OFFICIAL HANDBOOK OF THE INVINCIBLE UNIVERSE TP
ISBN: 978-1-58240-831-6
$12.99
INVINCIBLE PRESENTS, VOL. 1: ATOM EVE & REX SPLODE TP
ISBN: 978-1-60706-255-4
$14.99
THE COMPLETE INVINCIBLE LIBRARY, VOL. 1 HC
ISBN: 978-1-58240-718-0
$125.00
THE COMPLETE INVINCIBLE LIBRARY, VOL. 2 HC
ISBN: 978-1-60706-112-0
$125.00

THE WALKING DEAD

VOL. 1: DAYS GONE BYE TP
ISBN: 978-1-58240-672-5
$9.99
VOL. 2: MILES BEHIND US TP
ISBN: 978-1-58240-775-3
$14.99
VOL. 3: SAFETY BEHIND BARS TP
ISBN: 978-1-58240-805-7
$14.99
VOL. 4: THE HEART'S DESIRE TP
ISBN: 978-1-58240-530-8
$14.99
VOL. 5: THE BEST DEFENSE TP
ISBN: 978-1-58240-612-1
$14.99
VOL. 6: THIS SORROWFUL LIFE TP
ISBN: 978-1-58240-684-8
$14.99
VOL. 7: THE CALM BEFORE TP
ISBN: 978-1-58240-828-6
$14.99
VOL. 8: MADE TO SUFFER TP
ISBN: 978-1-58240-883-5
$14.99
VOL. 9: HERE WE REMAIN TP
ISBN: 978-1-60706-022-2
$14.99
VOL. 10: WHAT WE BECOME TP
ISBN: 978-1-60706-075-8
$14.99
VOL. 11: FEAR THE HUNTERS TP
ISBN: 978-1-60706-181-6
$14.99
VOL. 12: LIFE AMONG THEM TP
ISBN: 978-1-60706-254-7
$14.99
BOOK ONE HC
ISBN: 978-1-58240-619-0
$34.99
BOOK TWO HC
ISBN: 978-1-58240-698-5
$34.99
BOOK THREE HC
ISBN: 978-1-58240-825-5
$34.99
BOOK FOUR HC
ISBN: 978-1-60706-000-0
$34.99
BOOK FIVE HC
ISBN: 978-1-60706-171-7
$34.99
BOOK SIX HC
ISBN: 978-1-60706-327-8
$34.99
DELUXE HARDCOVER, VOL. 2
ISBN: 978-1-60706-029-7
$100.00
THE WALKING DEAD: THE COVERS, VOL. 1 HC
ISBN: 978-1-60706-002-4
$24.99

REAPER

GRAPHIC NOVEL
ISBN: 978-1-58240-354-2
$6.95

TECH JACKET

VOL. 1: THE BOY FROM EARTH TP
ISBN: 978-1-58240-771-5
$14.99

TALES OF THE REALM

HARDCOVER
ISBN: 978-1-58240-426-0
$34.95
TRADE PAPERBACK
ISBN: 978-1-58240-394-6
$14.95

TO FIND YOUR NEAREST COMIC BOOK STORE, CALL:
1-888-COMIC-BOOK

VALKING DEAD™, BRIT™ & CAPES™ © 2010 Robert Kirkman. INVINCIBLE ™ © 2010 Robert Kirkman and Cory Walker. BATTLE POPE™ © 2010 Robert Kirkman and Tony Moore. THE ASTOUNDING WOLF-MAN™ © 2010 Robert Kirkman and Jason Howar
TECH JACKET™ & CLOUDFALL™ © 2010 Robert Kirkman and E.J. Su. REAPER™ and © 2010 Cliff Rathburn. TALES OF THE REALM™ MVCreations, LLC. © 2010 Matt Tyree & Val Staples. HAUNT™ and © 2010 Todd McFarlane.
Image Comics® and its logos are registered trademarks of Image Comics, Inc. All rights reserved.